Blitz Kid

ELIZA GRAHAM

www.elizagraham.co.uk

Cover design by Carrie Kabak

For all in Oak Cottage.

ALSO BY ELIZA GRAHAM

Adult fiction

Playing with the Moon

Restitution

Jubilee

The History Room

ACKNOWLEDGEMENTS

My thanks to Maggie Dana and Carrie Kabak
in particular, and to everyone in the
Newplace writing group for their support.

1

If you think this is going to be about one kid's brave and patriotic actions during the Blitz, when the Germans were bombing London every night, this isn't the story for you. You'd be better off talking to the Girl Guides. I wasn't all that brave a lot of the time. And most people would say I wasn't all that patriotic, either.

It started with them trying to send me out of London.

The night I left, explosives were crashing down just streets away instead of crumping anonymously somewhere in the distance. My mother said the Germans were going to bomb the city into nothingness.

But I wasn't frightened.

I was furious.

* * *

Someone opened the railway carriage door where I sat waiting for the train to depart Liverpool Street Station. The scent of burning metal and hot bricks hit me like a slap in the face, mixing with the odour of damp clothes and fear. I scratched the sore bit on my cheek and began to count backwards from two thousand in nineteens.

A flare lit up the platform and I glimpsed travellers scurrying along the platform, faces taut and pale. The carriage door opened and the people inside shuffled up to let in the newcomers. 'Only another minute,' said a middle-aged man, slumping next to me. 'And we'll be out of this.' Everyone in the carriage sighed with relief. Except for me.

'Don't you worry, lovey,' said an old lady next to me. 'We'll soon be safe.' Fresh air and muddy hockey fields in an East Anglian boarding school, far, far away from danger. And from shops, cafés, libraries and cinemas.

I'd die of boredom in about three days. Or survive with a brain turned to porridge. And all the time I'd be worrying about my mother.

I shot up and tugged my suitcase out of the rack, hung my blasted gas mask round my neck, thrust open the carriage door and jumped down to the platform. The guard's whistle pursued me until the din of exploding bombs drowned it.

My suitcase felt as though it was full of rocks, but I managed to lug it across the station concourse until I found a quiet spot to think. Around me, people dragged luggage, parcels and children down to Underground platforms. My adrenalin ebbed away. The train ticket clutched in my hand seemed to burn my fingers. What had I done? There was going to be trouble. Trouble and I were old friends. We'd had fourteen years to get to know one another.

The concourse was empty now. Across the void the train I'd abandoned curled out of the station, like a fat worm burrowing into the earth. The light from the ticket office shone acid-drop green, making the darkness seem even inkier.

An explosion shook the floor. My nails cut like scissors into my palms. My breath came in gulps. I'd never felt like this before, so scared. So alive.

But the real fireworks would explode back at the flat when Mum saw I was home. Perhaps I could hide out somewhere in London, check up on her from time to time without her seeing me. But that was a daft idea. The boarding school would telegraph her to say I hadn't arrived. Better to go home and get the row over with. I had a ten-bob note in my pocket for tuck. More than enough to get me back to Fulton Street by taxi, providing a bomb didn't blow me up into tiny pieces.

Oh, God, please let there still be a taxi outside. If there was, it would be a sign I'd made the right decision.

A single cab was pulling away, its headlights thin yellow strips in the gloom. I waved at the driver and he braked.

'No more fares, miss,' he yelled. 'I'm going home now. It's bloody awful tonight.'

I tugged at the passenger door. 'Where's your home?'

'Off Goodge Street. Why?'

For once, luck was on my side. Goodge Street was only minutes from our flat. 'Drop me at the Tube station.' I jumped inside.

The cab driver shook his head. 'If you were my daughter . . .' The rest of his words were lost in the racket.

It took for ever for us to reach Goodge Street. The streets of the City of London, where all the banks are, were bad enough. But the raid grew even fiercer as we headed west. We took a detour up Gray's Inn Road, couldn't avoid a huge crater in what might have been Euston Road and had to work our way back south again. I think it was south, anyway. By then I felt completely lost. Sweat beaded the back of the driver's neck.

We made a back-street loop skirting the fire crews in Russell Square, explosions thumping around us and flares hissing overhead. I multiplied the numbers in the cab licence on the driver's dashboard by one another, fiddling with the coral bracelet on my wrist. The bracelet was rubbing against the sore skin, but I didn't want to take it off. My body was peppered with nasty red, itchy skin.

At last the driver halted outside the station.

'Get down to the platform quick, miss.' He refused the money I offered. 'You're off your trolley.'

It had been said before. Many times. By many different people. I just gritted my teeth and waved at him. A scream overhead made me lift my head to see a bomber, an engine on fire. The wounded plane, a Dornier, burned a scar across the night sky.

I wouldn't, couldn't, have been anywhere else but London.

Even though my mother was going to kill me.

2

'Stupid, ungrateful and immature!' Mum gave my shoulders a final shake and pushed me away. 'Even by your standards this is something else, Rachel.'

The floor rocked as a bomb went off but it didn't scare me as much as my mother's face. 'You've lost your mind!'

'I want to be with you. You need me.'

'I *need* not to be worrying about you. You'd have been safe at boarding school.'

'Yes, but then I'd have been worrying about *you*! You're not even down in the shelter.'

She let out a sigh that sounded like an angry rush of wind. 'If your father knew he'd be very upset.'

'Dad would understand.'

'He wants you to get an education, Rachel.' She had to shout above the thunderous noise outside.

'I can do my school work in the library. Like I've been doing already.' She'd have to admit I was conscientious about studying. Even French irregular verbs.

She shook her head, moving slowly into our living room as though underwater. 'There's nothing for you to eat except this stale bread.'

'I'll make toast.' I took off my coat, found plates, and sliced bread and some of the precious dripping from the scrawny piece of beef Mum had roasted last Sunday. The bombers weren't as loud now.

'You eat it for me, Rachel.' She pushed her plate towards me. I wanted to protest, but I was hungry. I always was these days. Sometimes my stomach would let out a hungry growl in the most embarrassing places: the library or the grocer's queue.

'I have to punish you.' She sounded sad. Mum had always hated punishments. 'You'll have to stay in your room all day tomorrow.'

I looked aside in case the pleasure showed on my face. She wasn't going to send me back to school.

After breakfast the next morning I sat on my bed, on top of the eiderdown. There was no room for a chair in my room. I had a couple of old used envelopes and a stub of pencil. Mum had forbidden me books for the day, but she hadn't said anything about not doing maths. So I multiplied seventeen by itself over and over again and tried to memorise the results. Numbers are what I turn to when I'm feeling bored, or under pressure or lonely or whatever else. Probably why I've never really got on with other girls my age. They like talking about lipstick – not that there's as much of that around now – and boys. Or other girls, in hisses and whispers.

I finished with the seventeens and started on a list of prime numbers: numbers that nothing divides into except themselves, zero and one. I felt like a prime number myself: something that nothing and nobody else really fitted into.

I jumped off the bed and peered at my face in the small mirror above the chest of drawers. The red patch on my cheek looked a little calmer this morning. I glanced down at my hands. The skin had flared up on them and was scaly and red. Lucky we'd reached the time of year when you could wear gloves most of the time. Some people even wore them indoors to save on heating fuel.

At lunchtime Mum brought me a cup of tea and a bowl of soup. She sat down on the bed next to me, her face drawn. We'd had so many chats before.

'Jumping off that train, Rachel. It was a silly thing to do. Illogical.'

'There was nothing illogical about it,' I told her. Any fool could work out the statistics of being killed in London. Even on the worst nights it was rare for more than, say, three thousand at most to die. The population of inner London was what, three or four million? Lots of people had left because of the bombs. That was just a one-in-a-thousand chance of dying.

I didn't point this out to Mum. She'd have said I was being like *that* again. She took my tray and left me alone.

At half-three she knocked on the door. 'I need you to go to the grocer's with the ration cards.'

It was a relief to be out in the fresh air again, even though the trip yielded nothing except two slices of ham so thin you could have read a book through them and a tin of carrots. We ate these for our supper. At least I did – Mum pushed hers around her plate. Then, just as she was telling me it was time to go down to the wretched Tube for the night, someone knocked on the door.

I opened it. Outside stood Mrs Hoffman, from the flat below us.

'*Ach du lieber Gott*, Rachel!' she shrieked. 'Weren't you on that train out of Liverpool Street last night?'

'I changed my mind.'

'Incendiaries hit it just outside London and there was a terrible fire. Many, many people died.' She put a hand to her mouth. My legs shook and my mouth felt dry.

Then Mum came out to see what was going on and Mrs H told her about the train and we were all hugging one another. I'd won the battle to stay in London.

3

The stray dog sniffed my shoes. I knew I ought to push him away, but something about him appealed to me. Perhaps it was the way his tail curled like a letter C. Or perhaps because he reminded me a bit of my own dog, Bounder: same kind of feathery coat and long legs. Except Bounder was a pedigree retriever and this mutt definitely wasn't. But Bounder belonged in the imaginary box I'd created marked '*Do Not Open*'.

I found half a stale biscuit in my raincoat pocket and held it out to the stray. He removed it with a courtier's delicacy and scuttled off a few yards in case I changed my mind. Dealing with animals is easy. They tell you what they want. I let the dog eat his biscuit and then whistled to him to come back.

'You're in luck, boy,' I told him, stroking his head. Only it was me who'd been in luck, escaping that train before it burned. I thought about the people who'd been in my carriage and shuddered.

The mongrel watched me as I unlocked my bike from the railings. Strictly speaking you weren't allowed to lock bikes to them, but who was going to complain *at a time like this*. People used that little phrase as a perfect excuse for doing just what they wanted. Or getting out of things they didn't want to do.

A day's work in the library beckoned. I was looking forward to it. As well as maths, of course, I was going to borrow the big world atlas and set myself the task of learning a map of Brazil, its principal rivers and mountains. I'd chosen Brazil because it seemed so glamorous and remote, with no rationing or air-raid shelters.

Before I could cycle off Mrs Hoffman opened the communal front door.

'Good morning, Rachel. How's your mother today?'

I studied the curlicues in the ironwork while I answered. 'She ate a piece of toast.' It had been the size of a stamp. 'And she's got another appointment at the hospital this afternoon.'

'I'll keep my fingers crossed. And what about you?' I could see her studying my sore cheek and scratched hands. She didn't say anything. Mrs H didn't go in for personal comments. If more people were like her we'd all be better off. 'Will your mother find you another school in London?'

'Don't know. Most of them have closed.' And Mum was wary of London schools. My last one had been blown to smithereens. No great loss to world civilisation in my view. I still enjoyed thinking of how the Luftwaffe had reportedly blasted the headmistress's filing cabinet with its drawers full of order marks and detention slips, many of them mine, into dust.

'Your mother may scold but she looks so happy to have you back, *liebchen*.'

'I want to help her.' Not that I could do much. I'd gone to schools that didn't believe in letting academically gifted girls, as they called us, learn cookery. But I could help with the cleaning and washing. And just *be* with her when she needed company. Even if it did mean nights down on that filthy Tube platform. 'I can help with the housework. And the shopping. It takes her hours to go shopping with the rationing.'

'Of course. You will be a great support to her.' Her gaze was still fixed on my hands. I wished I'd put on my gloves. 'That bracelet of yours is about to come off.'

'The catch needs fixing.' Dad had given me the coral beads for my birthday in June, just before everything started going badly wrong and we British turned from being defenders of the Poles and French into victims of aggression ourselves. I tugged the woollen gloves out of my pocket and put them on.

'That's right, keep warm. That was quite a frost last night.' Mrs H picked up her milk bottle and went inside. I jumped on my bike and pushed off in the opposite direction. The dog with the C-shaped tail sprang out of a doorway into the road and I swerved to avoid him.

I hadn't noticed someone crossing the road from the other side.

4

'Oi!'

I slammed on the brakes. The bike juddered to a halt, nearly launching me over the handlebars. The boy jumped back, dropping a black case which crashed on to the road.

'Sorry!'

'Why can't you bloody well look where you're going, silly cow.' His mouth was screwed into a scowl.

'I said I was sorry.' I propped up the bike against the kerb and went to pick up his case. A violin. 'Is it all right?'

He grabbed it from me and placed it carefully on the pavement to flip up the catches. We peered inside. I didn't know anything about musical instruments, but something about the way the violin's dark wood gleamed made me draw a breath. I put out a hand to touch its smooth surface.

He snapped down the lid. 'Hands off, nosey.'

'I'm not nosey.' We glared at each other. But I remembered I was really to blame for all this. 'Did I hurt you?'

He shook his head, picked up the case and started to walk away, his slim body tense. 'You should be in a bloody school, you should,' he called over his shoulder.

'So should you.' I said the first thing that came into my head.

He turned. 'I'm sixteen.'

'You don't look it.' In fact he did, but I wanted to rile him. Taking stabs at someone else is a relief, like scratching itchy skin.

'Bloody baby. Surprised your mummy lets you out alone.' He had a rough, deep voice and a pale face, out of which the most peculiar eyes – green, like a cat's – glinted. He was a cockney, probably from some slum.

'Don't let me keep you.' I used my old head-mistress's most dismissive tone.

'Snotty bint.' He strode off.

I could have hurled other taunts at his retreating back but it probably wasn't very dignified so I clamped my mouth shut and got back on my bike.

In the little square a block on from our street the frost had turned the grass into a silver cloth.

Even the bombed houses with their jagged facades seemed to complement the golds and coppers of the autumn leaves. The frosted, fractured houses looked like sad memorials to the way life used to be and could never be again.

And I would never again be that girl with the plaits who took riding lessons in Richmond Park, with a father who drove to his laboratory in London university each morning, and a healthy mother who played tennis with women called Cynthia and Amanda. Where we used to live in Putney was very respectable. Before the war lots of people had cars (even us) and took foreign holidays. I myself had once been to Brittany. We'd had a maid and a refrigerator and drank gin and tonic.

For a moment I forgot how dull that old life had been sometimes. It had been *our* life.

And people like that rude boy had had no part in it. I bit my lip hard because the cold air was making my eyes smart.

5

When I came back in the evening I couldn't help noticing what Mum called Fulton Street scruffiness: dustbins left out on the pavement, window boxes grown straggly and dusty. The red-bricked Victorian terraced houses could have been handsome if anyone bothered to polish the windows and sweep the stairs. The stray dog ran up the basement steps, sniffed the railings and cocked his head at me hopefully. I didn't have anything for him so he drifted away, turning to look at me every now and then as though hoping I'd suddenly produce a pork chop from my pocket.

As I walked inside Mum was on our landing talking to Mrs H.

'The doctor says they'll try to find me a bed but one of the wards was damaged last night. At least they're going to do *something*.' There was a desperate edge to her words.

I closed the front door as quietly as I could and tiptoed to the foot of the stairs.

'If only I could have persuaded Rachel to go to boarding school. She really shouldn't be in London.'

'Rachel's a young woman now. She likes the city.'

'Even with thousands of tons of explosives dropping down on it?'

'She is a great support to you, my dear.' I gave a silent cheer for Mrs H. Without meaning to, I moved slightly and a floorboard creaked.

'Who's there?' Mum called.

'Only me.' I called up, walking upstairs. She looked even paler this evening. 'How was your appointment?'

She was rearranging her expression into a cheerful smile. The result wasn't completely convincing. 'The consultant's hopeful.' I pretended to fiddle with the buckle on my satchel so she couldn't see the expression on my own face, which wouldn't have been convincingly cheerful, either. I could feel her gaze shift towards my raw hands.

'I put the cream on them.' I sounded defensive. 'It doesn't help.'

'The psyche plays a great role in balancing the body,' Mrs H said. 'When we're anxious we may manifest it physically.'

Mrs H said things like that occasionally. I put it down to her foreignness, but it was quite interesting, all the same.

'Clever Mrs Hoffman found us eggs for tea. And she even tracked down some bacon in the butcher's.' Did Mum know how false her voice sounded, all strained and jolly? 'Then you can go off to the shelter with your books.'

I didn't even bother arguing with her and went inside to bring the dry clothes off the fire escape. Technically it was an offence to block a fire escape with a clothes horse. Everything seemed to be an offence these days. But how else could you dry hand-washing if you lived in a flat with a tiny communal garden? Mum and I wouldn't have felt happy about displaying our smalls where Inspector Blake, who lived in the ground-floor flat, would see them right outside his sitting-room window.

When we'd finished the meal – if you can call a single egg and two stringy rashers of bacon a meal – Mum asked me if I'd had enough, just as she always did.

'Completely full,' I lied, just as I always did. When rationing first came in I was honest about saying I was always starving. She'd give me some of her own food, but then I noticed how hollow the little dip under each of her shoulder bones was growing. So after each meal I'd give my stomach a pat, the way Dad used to do after a big Sunday lunch. I knew it would really be growling for the buns the Women's Voluntary Service served down in the Tube.

I was still growing like crazy. Most of my old class had sprouted up years ago, but I'd waited until last summer. All my skirts were too short and most of my blouses were tight around the chest. I was a disaster area of a female: all gangly, my skin covered in red weals just in the worst places. I thanked God again that I wasn't confronting a gaggle of narrow-minded girls in that boarding school in the Fens. I'd found the people in my last school hard enough to understand and I'd had three years to get to know them. One or two girls had become kinder towards the end, just before the school was bombed. Perhaps the war had made them want to pull together. I even got invited to a birthday party. I think it was because someone else had whooping cough, though, and they wanted to make up the numbers.

Mum felt like a bit of air before the alert sounded and suggested I knock on Mrs H's door to see if she wanted to join us for a gentle stroll. We walked slowly downstairs, Mrs H and I trying not to show our alarm at how difficult Mum found the mild exercise. She moved like an old woman now, with frequent stops to catch her breath.

As we reached the ground floor the front door clicked open. Inspector Blake was home.

'Evening, ladies.' He tipped his trilby hat. The low evening sun showed up the lines round his eyes. He must once have been a jolly man. He didn't often laugh these days.

'How are the criminals, Inspector?' Mum asked 'I read about the looting up in Holloway. Terrible.'

'I thought people gave up crime in war,' I said. 'Uniting in a common cause, and all that.' I probably did sound a bit ironic when I said the last bit.

'Unfortunately not.' Inspector Blake gave his tight little smile. 'There've been about a dozen serious crimes committed just blocks away from here.'

'What kind of crimes?' I asked.

'Jeweller's shops raided in the blackout. Hospital dispensaries robbed of vital medicines.' He frowned. 'And there've been domestic robberies, too. A woman near here found someone had taken all the sheets off her bed while she was in the shelter.'

'Sheets?' Mum looked surprised.

'Five pounds a set. Worth stealing.'

Mum shook her head.

'A widow in New Cavendish Street came home to find all her children's toys had vanished during an air raid.' Perhaps he noticed how Mum's hand tightened on my arm because he paused. 'But please don't worry, Mrs Pearse, we'll get them.'

'How?' I asked.

'We're infiltrating the local gangs.'

It made me think of the Mafia in Chicago: raids on illegal drinking dens and nightclubs. But the London crime wave was happening in places like Holloway so it wouldn't be as glamorous. More like watching an old black-and-white film once you'd seen a glorious Technicolor movie.

A piercing whistle made us all jump. Perseus, Mrs H's budgerigar.

'*Liebchen!*' he called. '*Wo bist du?*'

'Ah.' Inspector Blake swallowed hard. 'Mrs Hoffman – '

'I must have left the cage uncovered again.' She sighed. 'He just can't forget those German words. And . . .' She looked away.

'It's nice for you to have someone speaking your own language.' The inspector's voice was kind. I could see the type of person he must have been before war and gangs took over his life. 'But when the window's open people hear that bird. A few comments have been made at the local station. Perhaps you could teach him some English expressions?'

'Up yours, Hitler,' I volunteered.

'Rachel!' Mum frowned at me. The siren wailed. 'No time for our walk after all. Fetch your things, darling, and get off to the Tube.'

'What about you?'

'I think I'd be better off tucked up in bed.' I knew she didn't like to be away from the bathroom and she couldn't get comfortable on the hard platform floor.

There was a steeliness to her expression that left me no choice but to run upstairs for the bedding left ready at the front door, next to my satchel. My gas mask, that wretched, clumsy object, was already hanging round my neck, ready to snag itself on railings or thump me in the chest.

'There's one man I've got my eye on,' Inspector Blake was saying as I trudged downstairs again. 'He's done well out of the war.'

I paused at the front door.

'Sounds as though you know them well,' Mum said.

'There's a pub just five minutes from here they like. Make sure you lock your doors when you go out and keep an eye on your valuables.'

'Rachel!' Mum called to me. 'Hurry up. If I find out you're dawdling on the streets, God help you.'

'I'll join you in a minute,' Mrs H said. 'When I've covered the bird and picked up my ID card and ration book.' We had to take all this stuff with us every night, just in case Hitler dropped one of his bombs on this building. Even though we'd had lots of practice now, it still took us more time than it ought to actually leave the house at the sound of the alert.

As for Inspector Blake, like most men he probably thought shelters were beneath his dignity, just for women and children.

I slammed the front door so hard that people on the street jumped, even with the siren wailing on and on.

6

I gave the dog with the C-shaped tail a bit of my lunchtime sandwich and rubbed my eyes, still sleepy after a disturbed night. He bolted it down as though I'd given him a marrowbone like the one Dad used to treat Bounder to on Saturdays. I knew I'd be starving again later on, but the dog looked so hungry.

'You can be fined or sent to prison for giving animals food fit for human consumption.'

That boy again. He was standing right behind me. I quickly shoved my hands into my pockets.

'It wasn't fit for human consumption. What's it to you?'

'Don't get your knickers into a twist.' He grinned. Good teeth – surprisingly straight and white. 'What was in that sandwich?'

'The grocer says it's ham but if it's been any-where near a pig I'm Hitler's niece.'

'Probably a bit of badger.' He rooted in his pocket. 'Have a bit of this.' He produced a bar of Cadbury's. I stared at the familiar purple wrapper. 'You can still get it if you know where to look.' I had a feeling that accepting his chocolate would be something I'd regret, but I couldn't resist reaching out to break off a square and place it in my mouth. It melted on my tongue and I could hardly bear to swallow it. My eyes watered because it reminded me of my father. He'd always buy me Cadbury's after we'd collected Bounder's marrowbone from the butcher's on Saturday mornings.

I scratched my cheek.

The boy was watching me.

'What's wrong? Not good enough for you? Expect you like boxes of chocolates done up in satin ribbon.' He sounded amused.

'It's lovely. It just made me think of someone.'

He raised an eyebrow. 'Boyfriend?' That was a joke: me, Rachel Pearse, with a boyfriend?

'*Nein, nein, nein,*' Perseus shouted from the floor above. Mrs H must have pulled up the window sash to air the room. I hoped this boy hadn't made out the German words.

'It reminded me of my dad.'

'Likes to treat you, does he?' He sounded interested rather than inquisitive.

'I haven't seen him for months.'

The boy said nothing but shoved the chocolate back at me. I took another square.

'Your dad in the forces, is he?'

'He does special work somewhere secret out of town.' Mum could never tell me much about what Dad was up to and didn't like talking about it. It was classified or something. Important, anyway. The boy kept watching me with his cat's eyes. 'What's your name?' I asked, to distract myself from thoughts of Dad.

'Gabriel. Paul Gabriel.'

Like the Angel Gabriel. Only he didn't look angelic. But not quite like a devil, either.

'My mum named me after St Paul.' Was he having me on? 'What about you?'

'Rachel.' I didn't give my surname. 'Named after nobody in particular.'

He repeated it. I couldn't tell whether he thought it was a good name or not. Then his eyes seemed to catch a glimpse of something further down the street and he muttered to himself and ran off. I was almost relieved.

Inspector Blake was on his way home, reaching into his overcoat pocket for the front door keys.

'Evening, Rachel.'

'Evening.'

'That young fellow.' He pointed down the street in the direction Paul Gabriel had taken. 'Do you know him?'

'I've talked to him a couple of times.'

'He's a bad sort.' The inspector sounded testy. Mind you, most people did after so many disturbed nights. 'Don't get friendly with him.' He made an effort to brighten his expression. 'Ready for the shelter?'

'Yes.' All I had to do was get the supper and there wasn't enough food for that task to take much time.

'And you still think London's better than boarding school?' He smiled so fleetingly I almost wondered if I'd imagined it.

'Who wouldn't?'

'You didn't like school?'

I remained silent. How to explain order marks for asking perfectly normal questions? Silly girls giggling about boys? Pointless drill in the playground?

'My boy, Edmund, enjoyed his school. Keen on sport, you see. Particularly cricket.' The inspector hadn't mentioned his family before.

'Where is he now?' Stupid question – he was probably in some training camp.

He looked down at his shiny shoes. 'He was on the *Royal Oak*.'

The Germans had sunk that ship at the beginning of the war. Pretty well everyone had drowned. 'I'm sorry.' But the inspector's mind already seemed to have switched to other matters.

'Things disappear when young Gabriel's around,' he said.

Funny, that. I *had* been missing something: my coral bracelet. I hadn't seen it since yesterday morning when I'd collided with Paul Gabriel.

'You said something about gangs of thieves operating round here?' I tried to sound only politely interested.

'I certainly did.'

'Which pub did you say they met at?'

'I didn't.' He looked at his watch.

I thought quickly, trying to remember their names and locations. There was one particularly grimy one I'd passed on the way to Charing Cross Road to visit the bookshops. What was its name?

'The Blue Lion?' I asked innocently.

The inspector's head gave a jerk. 'Stay away from that place.' His eyes were suddenly sharp. 'London's dangerous these days and I don't just mean because of the bombs.'

Words to ignite my curiosity.

7

Once again Mum didn't turn up at our usual refuge on the Tube platform, but Mrs H appeared and sat with me beside the fire bucket.

'Your mother thought it would be easier for everyone if she stayed in the house,' she said, settling herself on her bedding. She meant that Mum was in too much pain to leave the flat.

What a night it was. Not the bombs (though they were noisy enough), but the man in merchant sailor's uniform and his girlfriend. It was like a sex-education lesson. At least I learned things I hadn't known before, despite keeping my eyes averted. I tried not to listen to what was going on, but it was hard not to. Someone even clapped when they'd finished.

Mrs H said it was always interesting to ask oneself why people needed to exhibit themselves. She said there was often a psychological reason, going back to childhood. Possibly premature potty training. Continentals talk frankly about sex and bodily functions. I would not have learned about this kind of thing at boarding school. They would have given us more diagrams of the reproductive system to copy. The reproductive system of a flower, that is.

The people around us on the platform gawked at Mrs H while she related her potty-training theory and I wished, disloyally, that she didn't have such a clear voice and a German accent. But a few of them probably learned a few things, so you could argue that it was a kind of public service.

The rest of the time I let my mind drift to the Blue Lion pub and that boy who might have stolen my bracelet. We were back in Mrs H's flat by the early hours of the next morning so at least we had some sleep.

By the following evening I knew I'd have to go to the pub.

I'd spent the afternoon going through my wardrobe looking for something to wear that didn't scream *schoolgirl*. That makes it sound as though there were plenty of clothes to choose from. In fact, I'd outgrown most of what I had. I gave up in despair and raided Mum's wardrobe while she had a nap in the living room, borrowing a silk blouse she rarely wore. I fiddled with my hair so that I looked, I hoped, more like the film star Veronica Lake and a little less like a schoolgirl, a lock of hair falling over my forehead. I had a search around in Mum's dressing table for something for my lips. I'd despised girls at my old school who'd blathered on for hours about clothes and make-up. As I attempted lipstick for the first time I wished I'd paid more attention to what they'd said. It took several goes before I looked more like a sophisticated female and less like a clown. Lipstick is good at getting on to places you wouldn't want it to go, such as your teeth or cheeks. And it's hard to rub it off.

I kissed Mum goodbye and let her think I was going straight to the shelter. It was dark in the living room and she didn't notice my hair or the lipstick. Her lack of attention might also have been because of the pain. The hospital had finally set a date for the operation. They wanted to admit her tomorrow. It seemed terribly sudden and I suspected Mum had known for a while and thought I'd be out of the way at school when she was admitted. While she was away I was going to sleep at Mrs H's. I could have kicked up a fuss and insisted on sleeping in our own flat, but I was worried about further threats of boarding school.

I walked past shop fronts with blistered paintwork and smeared windows, criss-crossed with tape. Most people would have considered this area grotty, but I didn't mind. It fascinated me. Mum and I had washed up here when we left Putney. We chose Fitzrovia because it was near Dad's old university lab, which made us feel as though we were still near him somehow. But walking past his old workplace made me sad. I couldn't help imagining that he was still working away up on the third floor and might even look out of the window and wave. As if this would even have been possible with the blackout blinds pulled down.

Half-six. The evening siren had already wailed at us. Bombers on the way. I'd promised Mum I'd go straight to the shelter. That's the kind of person I was: a breaker of promises. But I couldn't face the platform just now. You might as well be buried alive as spend a whole night down there. I looked over my shoulder, towards the south-east. No bombers just yet. Mrs H would ask me why I'd taken so long.

I also wished I hadn't read what I'd read just before I'd left the flat, when I'd been rifling through the pile of books and magazines by the sofa, looking for some scrap paper to use for writing out equations. Mum must have borrowed a family medical encyclopaedia from the library. She'd inserted a small corner of an envelope between two of the pages: a scrap so small she must have thought I wouldn't notice it. Or perhaps she'd assumed I'd be safely away at school while she was researching and hadn't had the time or strength to return the book to the library.

I scanned the words on the pages. '*Loss of weight without a weight reduction diet an important symptom . . . abdominal pain occurring later on . . . Anaemia . . . Surgery may be successful in cases diagnosed promptly.*'

I flicked through to the start of the section. It was under 'C'. C for cancer. A disease I had been trying not to think of where Mum was concerned. But I wasn't going to brood on that word now. I was going to place the cancer in the '*Do Not Open*' box.

As I approached Windmill Street doubt made me slow my pace. What was I trying to do? I should report my stolen bracelet to the inspector instead of coming to this grubby pub to confront the thief. One of the things about growing older is that you sometimes step back and see yourself from a distance. You note, quite coolly, what you really want from a situation. Which isn't always what you tell yourself you want.

Even if Paul Gabriel was here tonight I had no idea how he'd react if I accused him of stealing the bracelet. He'd almost certainly just deny it outright. Of course he would, he was a rough boy from a rough part of London. A thief, almost certainly, just as Inspector Blake claimed.

I'd never been in a pub by myself. Before Hitler had stamped his way into Poland and started the war Mum and Dad would sometimes take me to inns by the river in Richmond or Maidenhead. We'd sit in the garden and I'd have ginger beer and a packet of crisps. Dad would have a pint of best and Mum would have gin and tonic. The Blue Lion didn't look like one of those riverside pubs. The pavement was littered with cigarette butts. Every time someone opened the door the stink of beer and fags and something I preferred not to identify wafted out.

I started to walk away. A man in a green tweed coat with a pig-faced white dog raised his hat to me as he passed me. I gave a half-nod in answer and went on down the street until I reached a poster pasted to the wall. It showed a woman's eyes. 'LET YOUR EYES GET USED TO THE BLACK-OUT.' I didn't mind the blackout. I seemed to find my way round by instinct. Perhaps I was really a night creature, with eyes adjusted for the murky environment. A night creature, not some milksop schoolgirl. So why not go back to that pub? A bomb might get me tonight. Or Mum might die, let's face it – she might. Then I'd be sent off to some ghastly institution and I wouldn't have this opportunity again.

I retraced my steps. As I pushed open the pub door men turned to stare. I stepped inside, letting the door swing shut and wishing I was wearing something more sophisticated over the silk blouse than an old school raincoat which was at least two inches too short and a shabby navy beret. And that I wasn't carrying the rolled blanket, damn silly schoolgirl's satchel and the wretched gas mask that Mum insisted I took everywhere. At least my too-revolting chapped hands were masked by thin kid leather gloves instead of the woollen ones.

My eyes strained to pick out figures through the smoke. Paul Gabriel was standing at the bar. Surely he was too young to be served? I glanced over my shoulder, half expecting Inspector Blake to be there. When I looked back at the bar, Paul Gabriel himself was staring at me. I arranged my features into what I hoped was a look of mild, ironic surprise.

'We meet again,' I said.

'What are you doing here?'

He didn't seem either surprised or particularly pleased to see me here. Mildly amused, if anything.

'I just came in to buy a box of matches.' I made my way towards him, accidentally shoving my rolled-up blanket into a middle-aged woman with very black hair, who glared at me through heavily made-up eyes.

'Didn't notice you were a smoker.'

I felt my cheeks colouring and longed to give the sore patch of skin on the left one a good scratch. 'It's for my emergency pack. Torch, whistle, blankets, water, candles . . .'

'Don't light up until you're sure the gas mains haven't been blown,' offered the landlord as he handed me a box of Swan Vestas. 'You'll blow yourself up and save Jerry the trouble.' Paul Gabriel passed him a coin in payment.

'Thank you, but I couldn't possibly . . .' I was all flustered.

'Want a drink?'

He knew I'd come in here to find him. I shook my head and sat down on the bar stool, both at the same time.

'Well . . . a shandy. Thank you.' I wondered if the landlord would let me have it as it was half beer, but he didn't raise an eyebrow. I put down my things and brushed an invisible hair off the raincoat collar. Perhaps Mum's Elizabeth Arden lipstick had done the trick. I hoped so, because if she found out I'd helped myself to it I'd never hear the end of it. Only, of course, she'd soon be in hospital and probably wouldn't need make-up.

I pushed this thought out of my mind and took my drink from Paul Gabriel, trying hard not to drop it because the leather gloves made my hands slippery. The glass didn't look too clean, but I didn't want to risk appearing fussy so I drank up. Last time I'd had a shandy had been a special treat with Mum and Dad in a pub garden just before the war had started. 'Don't get used to drinking alcohol, young lady,' Dad had warned me. I'd wished I'd just ordered a plain lemonade as I didn't really like the flavour the beer added to the drink. But this evening the shandy tasted just fine.

Outside the siren wailed. Nobody inside made any signs of moving to the shelters.

'Is this a regular haunt of yours?' I asked. Now he really *would* think I was interested in him. To calm myself down I silently recited the seventeen times tables.

'Suppose it is. My business keeps me on the move.' The landlord gave a slight cough and picked up his cloth, dabbing at one of the taps. The pub didn't look exactly spotless. The lino could have used a mop and the bar was sticky with beer slops.

'What do you do?' I hoped I only sounded casually interested, nothing more. He was just a boy, after all. He couldn't have a business.

'Pick things up, sell them on, that kind of thing.' He sipped his half of watery-looking bitter. His hands were long and slender for a criminal's. Usually they have stubby palms and squat fingers. According to the books, at least.

'Sounds interesting. What kind of things?'

'Bits and pieces. Jewellery, artworks, musical instruments. Like that violin you saw me with the other day.'

'When I nearly ran you over.' I stared at him, looking for traces of guilt about the bracelet. Nothing. I sipped my lemonade. I'd drink up and get out of here.

He stared back at me, innocent, blank. 'I can get lipstick and rouge, too, you know. And face powder.' My hand went to my nose. Mum always told me I was far too young for powder. 'What do you use?' he asked. 'Yardley or Coty? I could add you to my client list.'

His *client list.* What kind of people would be on that? But what did I have to lose?

'Yes, do add me. A light shade.' Or else Mum would notice and there'd be trouble.

'What's your surname?'

'Pearse, Rachel Pearse.'

'I'll keep my eyes open for you so's I can let you know when I've got it.'

I'd been dismissed. I felt half annoyed and half relieved, even though I hadn't really accomplished what I'd come here to do.

I stood and picked up all my stuff. 'Thank you. And thanks for the drink.' He nodded and went back to his beer. As soon as I was out of earshot he and the barman would be making crude comments about me. What a fool I'd made of myself. And I'd never even got round to asking about my lost bracelet.

Outside the pub the air felt so chilly it was like jumping into a cold bath. My hands pleaded with me to scratch them so I pulled off the leather gloves. I put down the rolled-up blanket and pulled my own wool gloves out of my pocket. They'd be warmer than the leather ones. Something came out with the gloves, something bright and circular. My bracelet: snagged on the wool. It must have been here in my pocket all the time.

The pub door thudded. Someone had followed me outside.

'Why'd you really come here, Rachel?' Paul Gabriel's green eyes were screwed up in suspicion. I could lie, repeat the line about the matches, but I didn't. This evening had gone completely wrong, so why not just be honest about my suspicions.

'I thought you'd stolen this.' I showed him the bracelet. He took it from me gently. Above us a couple of planes droned and a gun opened fire.

'Nice, delicate bit of work. You wouldn't get much for it. Silver and gold's what they want these days. And diamonds. Always popular, diamonds.' He didn't seem put out that I'd accused him of theft. Perhaps he was used to accusations. He handed the bracelet back to me and I tried to replace it in my pocket with the palms of my hands held upwards so he couldn't get a good glance at my eczema, even if he'd been able to, in the blackout. 'Who's told you what about me?' he asked, his eyes daring me to be honest.

'In our flats there's an Inspector Blake.' A flash of recognition from Paul Gabriel. 'He saw you talking to me.'

He kicked out at the brickwork on the pub wall.

'Bloody cop! He follows me everywhere.' The first bomb landed. Not too close. Yet.

'He says you steal things. Do you?' I raised my voice now against the din. I don't know what possessed me to throw this accusation at him.

Paul Gabriel scowled. 'Let me ask *you* a question.' He was shouting and his voice shook just a little. 'Why are you still in London? Why aren't you somewhere safe with the rest of the kiddies?'

'I'm not a kid!'

He took both my wrists and shook them. I tried not to grimace as he touched the sore bits. I felt the vibrations of the bombers underneath the soles of my feet on the pavement.

'Yes, you are. A silly little girl, with your ideas about people and your cop friends.' He let me go.

'My mother's got cancer. That's why we're still here.' I blinked, hardly believing I'd said that word. It had only been a few hours since I'd first stared at it. 'I can't leave her alone.'

I'd taken too much of a risk: exposed a weakness he could use against me. I turned and ran for the shelter.

8

Metal fragments from a crashed bomber littered our street next morning and the reek of aviation fuel hung over us.

'A Dornier came down in the square,' Inspector Blake said as he and I collected our bottles of milk from the front doorstep. 'It's still there.'

It must have come down shortly after my confrontation with Paul Gabriel so perhaps it was as well I'd gone straight from seeing him to the shelter. The all-clear hadn't sounded until well past midnight. I'd been half-asleep as we walked home and hadn't noticed the metal shards.

On our way home from settling Mum into the hospital Mrs H and I made a detour to look at the German plane. Already some urchins had helped themselves to bits and pieces from the cockpit, ignoring the police signs warning people not to go near the plane. A group of Boy Scouts raked the grass for any bits of metal still left from the pillaging. The bare legs beneath their short uniform trousers looked blue in the cold air.

'Come on, *liebchen*.' Mrs H sounded sad. An elderly woman pushing a wicker trolley shot her an evil look. Mrs H was probably thinking about the pilot, her countryman, who'd been killed in the crash. It was strange to think of a Luftwaffe pilot as being human, too, with family and friends who might be mourning him now. Every time we shot a plane down, Mrs H probably wondered if the crew were sons of people she'd once known in Germany. 'I bought mushrooms in Berwick Street market this morning,' she went on, in a brighter tone. 'And a rabbit. We'll make a stew for supper.'

She cheered up even more when we were back in her kitchen, dissolving Marmite in boiling water to use as stock and throwing in a couple of cold boiled potatoes left over from the previous night to thicken the stew, along with a handful of herbs I didn't recognise. Continentals are very keen on herbs. The results looked very foreign when she ladled me out a generous portion, but tasted rich and earthy and warmed me up inside. Except in that part that would probably never feel entirely warm again until my family was safely reunited. If that ever happened.

I had seconds. For pudding we had baked apples filled with the few-remaining sultanas Mrs H had put aside last Christmas. She was trying to cheer me up with as good a supper as she could muster. And it was working: I certainly felt fuller than I had for weeks. Tonight, perhaps, my stomach wouldn't rumble while I waited for the buns to be served on the platform.

Perseus had a treat too, a piece of ragged lettuce leaf she'd begged from a stallholder. I pushed it between his bars.

'*Danke!*' he squawked and rang his bell twice before attacking the green leaf with his sharp beak.

'Say "Thank you" like an English budgie,' I urged him, but he was too busy eating his lettuce to bother with lessons.

Mrs H sat back in her chair. 'I like having someone to cook for,' she said. 'If only I still had the pots and pans we left behind in Berlin. I miss them still. I wonder if they would let me bring some soup into the ward for your mother. She needs good, nourishing food.'

Mum had looked as grey as a slice of National Loaf bread this afternoon. Now that we'd finished the cooking and eating I had time to worry about her.

The operation had been put off until tomorrow because they still hadn't patched up the damaged operating theatre. At least Mum was comfortable:

they'd given her something for the pain. Mrs H worried about medicines. Or lack of them. She was convinced all the drugs were going to the military. I didn't like thinking about this so I began cubing the number three to distract myself. Three times three is nine. Times three is twenty-seven. Times three is eighty-one. Times three is . . .

Mrs H was telling me to collect my things, it was nearly time for the alert. I had to stop my mental sums. The image of my mother in terrible pain followed me like an evil shadow as I prepared for the shelter, gathering my blanket, gas mark and satchel together and following Mrs H out on to the dark street towards the Tube station. Perhaps Mum would die and Dad would never return from his secret work. I'd left be an orphan, like Jane Eyre, or Pip in *Great Expectations*, or Mary in *The Secret Garden*. Child heroes were usually orphans. Once, living in Putney in our comfortable family home, I'd worried that my parented state had ruled me out of a life of adventure. Now I wished I hadn't been so damn silly. The old pre-war life might have had its boring parts, but it hadn't given me that cold feeling in my stomach that even Mrs H's stew could only temporarily shift.

We reached our usual spot on the platform and arranged our bedding. Mrs H pulled out her needles and carried on with the socks she was making for men on Atlantic convoys. Mr H had been locked up by this country for no other reason than for having a German passport, but Mrs H was never bitter about this. She just carried on with her knitting for our merchant sailors. Sometimes I felt like marching to Number Ten Downing Street, hammering on the door and letting them all know what I thought about that.

But there was something about the rhythmic clicking of the needles that soothed me out of these scared and angry thoughts. Things could actually be worse, far worse. I wasn't an orphan and I was having adventures. Mr H wasn't in one of those brutal German camps where they beat up the inmates. Even though I was always hungry I wasn't actually starving to death.

Any minute now I'd sound so much like Pollyanna I'd make myself sick.

I looked around the platform. Far less grotty down here now than when we first started sheltering in the Tube. We had proper lavatories so people didn't have to relieve themselves on the rails, which was truly disgusting. I sometimes had a feeling that some of those sheltering down here enjoyed it a bit too much. Tatterdemalions, that's what they called them, people who lived underground for days, even weeks, at a time. Troglodytes, more like, cave-dwellers who only surfaced for a few hours in the daylight, reeking of body odour. And worse.

I hoped Mrs H and I didn't smell when we'd been down here. Mrs H was very clean, possibly even cleaner than my mother, who until now had been the most fastidious person I'd known.

You weren't allowed deep baths in wartime as heating up all that water used up too much fuel. I missed deep soaks with bath essence and one of Mum's *Tatler*s to read. Even if Mum didn't like me immersing myself for too long, saying the water was bad for my skin. At least thinking of the rose-scented bath essence helped take my mind off the stink down here, even if it did make me itch.

Mrs H gave a little snore. She'd fallen asleep over the sock, her mouth slightly open. I retrieved the needles and pulled her blanket over her chest. A last train announced its melancholy arrival in the station, windows boarded over so the blackout would be preserved when the carriages surfaced again. Quieter overhead tonight. The bombers must be further out, perhaps east over the docks. I thought of the firemen trying to douse the flames, of crashing timbers, flaming warehouses filled with precious sugar. Did burning sugar smell like toffee? It seemed frivolous even to wonder.

I could have read, using my blackout torch, but my mind kept darting round, dwelling on those things I'd rather not think about. Even a page of equations wouldn't have soothed me now. I needed new mathematical tricks. I needed someone to teach me more advanced algebra. The skin on the banks of my hands felt dry and tight. Resisting the urge to scratch it was torture.

I needed to be out of here.

Temptation crept into my mind. It depended on the warden, though. Sometimes he went for a mug of cocoa at about this time. If he wasn't standing at the top of the escalator I could slip out of the station for half an hour, get some air. If it turned heavy I'd come back. A faint pang of guilt hit me. I was supposed to be acting maturely and not taking silly risks. I knew Mum didn't entirely trust me. Not just because I'd jumped off the train at Liverpool Street. She would have remembered the other things I'd done when I was younger: climbing through the cloakroom window at my junior school to get out of doing physical training, or pretending to faint during boring church services so I could read novels in the sanatorium instead.

The pang didn't last long. And something or someone was on my side this evening because I eased up all the hundred steps leading to the ticket office and out onto the inky street without being stopped. In the distance planes rumbled. Now and then searchlights seared the sky, picking out black swarms overhead. The barrage balloons swung like giant silver party decorations. To the east a big white cloud billowed, snowy round the edges but turning grey, then amber, and finally flickering with livid red at its core. Sometimes I felt guilty at finding the Blitz beautiful.

Three girls in evening dresses and fur tippets tumbled past on the arms of young officers, all of them oblivious to the searchlights and thumping of the bombs to the east. They'd probably sail down Tottenham Court Road to a restaurant, and then on to Leicester Square to laugh in the back rows of the cinema, or drink in the Kit-Cat Club in Regent Street. I knew about these places from Mum's magazines. The girls only looked about seventeen, even with their rouge and red lipstick. Not much older than I was. I knew that was one reason Mum wanted me to go to school in the dull old country: to escape the poor example of females throwing themselves at Our Gallant Boys. But tonight, in the light of the flares and explosions, these boys and girls looked like young gods and goddesses. Even the short officer with spots, and the girl with badly dyed blonde hair.

Something moved to my left and I jumped. A woman, older than the dressed-up girls, almost as old as Mum, emerged from an alleyway, brushing down her tight skirt and smoothing her waved hairstyle. I looked away. Seconds later a man in private's uniform strode past me, head bowed towards the pavement. I knew I was blushing and I'm pretty sure he was too.

I was a long way from being the awkward little schoolgirl with the plaits I'd been at the start of the war. But when I thought about sex and men I felt as if I was drifting on a dark sea and nobody could tell me where I'd end up.

I wasn't concentrating on where I was going. Which was silly because suddenly anti-aircraft fire burst out. The swarm of bombers was directly over me, illuminated by the searchlights for a split second. And there I was, out in the open. Panic immobilised me. My legs weren't working. Gunfire crackled again. A bomb landed a block away and the buildings around me shook. An incendiary dropped into the gutter beside me. I stared at the smoking metal cylinder, not even capable of putting it out.

A foot stamped on it. Someone took my arm.

'Let's get inside.'

Paul Gabriel.

9

'Quick.' He dragged me across the road and down a set of concrete steps into a basement. A flare lit up the sky and I saw his face: pale and intent. I stumbled on the last step and for a moment he took my full weight as though I were a small child. He had strong muscles for such a thin boy.

He let me go and pulled away the boards from the door.

'They didn't do much of a job shutting up when they left for the country.' I could barely hear him. He put his shoulder to the door and it opened, revealing a passageway. 'In you go.'

He slammed the door behind us and the roaring and crashing quietened. My ears started to recover.

'How do you know about this house?'

'A friend told me about it.' He looked away. 'That's my job, knowing things like this.'

He glanced over his shoulder as though someone else might have followed us in. 'We can sit here in the kitchen.'

He pulled a torch out of his pocket and shone the beam to show me the table and chairs. We sat down, perching on the edges of our seats as though we were about to be interrogated. I thought again about my statistics. A one-in-a-thousand chance of dying. But the figures were far worse if you were directly under the Heinkels and Dorniers. As we were now.

The bombs still thundered around us, but Paul seemed to relax back into his chair. Gradually I felt myself lose some of the tension in my own shoulders. If death was going to come for me now there wasn't much I could do about it. Foolish to run for the shelter. We didn't say anything for the next five minutes. It didn't seem necessary. Our eyes met. Paul's expression was slightly quizzical. He still couldn't make me out. I couldn't make myself out, either, a lot of the time. Paul stood up.

'C'mon. I'll show you round. It'll take your mind off it.' He sounded as though this were his own place. I followed him along a black-and-white-tiled passage and upstairs to the ground floor, the route the servants must once have taken, bearing trays of food. He opened a door off to the right of the hallway and switched on the light. The windows were blacked out so there was no risk of arousing the wrath of the air-raid warden. Someone had covered the sofas with dust sheets but he pushed them aside so we could sit down.

'I hope Mrs Hoffman doesn't wake up and find me gone.'

'Who's she?'

I told him.

'Another five minutes and you can run back.' He sounded so confident, as though the German air force would do as Paul Gabriel wished. 'Jerry dropped most of his bombs over the docks, he hasn't got much left.' The roaring above us had indeed quietened and the explosions were fewer now. He hadn't asked me what on earth I'd been doing, wandering around by myself in a raid. I was grateful. But he was watching me again. 'You ever play truth or dare, Rachel Pearse?'

So my suspicions of him were justified. He'd rescued me but now there was a price to pay. Or a challenge to meet.

'Yes.' The word seemed to come from deep inside me.

'What kind of dares were they?'

My throat was dry. 'Oh, silly things.'

'Like?'

'Can't remember.'

'Bet you can really.'

'Which boys you liked, you know, that kind of thing.' I could still smell the hot tar surface of the playground at my junior school in the summer term, the gang of boys and girls around me, daring me. Back then I'd had a certain notoriety – I'd take on almost any dares, not always understanding that some were better left untaken.

'And is there a boy you want, truth or dare?' His green eyes still threw out their challenge.

I couldn't answer. I had to leave. It was as though the oxygen in the room had escaped. But the front door would doubtless be locked. I doubted I could get down to the basement and out that way before he caught me. The thought scared me. And thrilled me. I closed my eyes and began squaring four.

'Where do you go when you do that?' He sounded interested.

I opened my eyes. 'What do you mean?'

'You do something in your head. You go somewhere. Does it calm you down?'

I nodded. 'It's numbers. I like them. I like the patterns.' I waited for him to start mocking me, but he didn't.

'You never answered my question. Which boy do you want?'

'I'll take the dare.' I sounded composed.

'Very brave. Or maybe not.' He studied me. 'So this is the dare. Nick something from this house.'

'Nick something?'

'Pinch something. Steal it.' He waved a hand, dismissing my gasp. 'Nobody'll see. It's dark.'

'You can't be serious?'

'You know the rules of the game.'

'But it's . . .'

'Looting, I know.' He winked at me. 'Doesn't have to be valuable. A candle. A pencil stub. A comb.' He waved towards the drawing-room door.

I went back downstairs to find the kitchen, half expecting to hear a shout or a whistle from a warden or policeman. I was about to become a looter, a thief, one of those people Inspector Blake hunted down. These days they could hang you for looting. I wasn't sure whether they'd do that to someone who wasn't quite fifteen, but I imagined they'd have other unpleasant ways of punishing you. I bent down and scratched behind my knee, nerves making my skin prickle.

Suppose this was just a trap? Suppose Paul Gabriel planned on letting himself out and boarding up the basement again, leaving me shut up here alone to bang on the windows and scream for help from the warden, who'd summon the police to arrest me. But I knew Paul wouldn't do this. He was testing me. He'd want to see the results of this expedition.

I crept along the tiled passageway, the darkness deepening. Luckily I had my blackout torch. A door opened up to the right: some kind of pantry.

As well as the white stone sink and empty shelves, I made out the rectangular shape of a canvas-wrapped object about three foot tall and two foot wide propped up against the wall. A painting?

I undid the strings holding the canvas together and pulled it down. A girl's fair hair shone out from a gilt frame. Her lips were full and red. She held a mirror to her face, eyebrows slightly raised, as though she was uncertain what she thought of her reflection. A white-and-copper spaniel draped its silky head over her slippers. Unobserved, a young man stood in a doorway studying her, a frown on his face. Years ago Dad had taken me to the National Gallery and this oil reminded me of the paintings in the Dutch Rooms. She put me in mind of something – someone – else, too. Of myself: this painted girl was a more perfect, unblemished, blonder me. Me as I might be if I didn't have irritated skin and wore silks and velvet instead of outgrown kids' clothes.

A pantry seemed a strange place to store something so beautiful. But perhaps the owners of the house thought it would be safer down here during the raids. For a moment I toyed with the idea of lugging it upstairs to Paul Gabriel. That would surprise him, wouldn't it? But the thought of stealing something so nearly matching my own image felt peculiar. And besides, this painting must be valuable. I smoothed the canvas back over the painting, re-tied the strings and went back into the corridor.

I still hadn't taken anything. I was about to give up and tell him I'd tell the truth instead of carrying out the dare when my nose caught the scent of something familiar. I squinted through the shadows and made out the shape of roses, long-stemmed and blood-red, dried out, the water all evaporated from the crystal vase. What a penny-romance thing to steal. I couldn't take one of the flowers: he'd think I had a crush on him. Perhaps there'd be an old dishcloth in the kitchen. Nobody would miss something like that.

Something warm and furry brushed against me. I stifled a scream. A flare outside brightened the room a degree and I glimpsed a cat at my legs. It must have followed us into the house. Time to get the hell out. I pulled off my woollen glove, plucked a single stem from the vase and ran upstairs to the drawing room, the cat pitter-pattering behind me.

Paul Gabriel was still sitting where I'd left him.

'Rotten of them to leave their cat when they went.' I tried to keep my voice even as I handed over the dead rose. He placed it carefully in his lap, looking it over.

'Probably ran off during a raid and got lost.' The creature rubbed itself against his legs. Paul stroked it in long movements from between its ears to the end of its back. Again I noticed how slender his hands were. 'This the best you could do?' He nodded down at the rose.

'It was that or a dishcloth.' I decided to take control of the situation, attack before he could. 'My turn to ask the questions. Why did you bring me here? Was it just to get me out of the raid? Truth or dare?'

'Truth. I wanted to see if you're what I think you are.'

'What's that?'

'Just another goody-goody middle-class girl. Or someone with a bit of spark to her.'

'Do I pass the test?'

For a while I thought perhaps he hadn't heard the question. Then he nodded. 'You're like me. This war's freed you, let you do things you wouldn't have done before it started.'

'Yes.' It was true. It made me guilty, acknowledging that war suited me.

'Don't feel bad about it.'

'I can't help wondering ...'

'What?'

'My mother's so ill and people are dying in this city every night. While I'm enjoying myself. Most of the time. I shouldn't be finding the Blitz exciting, should I?'

He said nothing but again I felt something, a warmth, a sympathy, coming from him.

'I lost my mum and dad when I was a little kid. My gran brought me and my sister up. Till she died, too. Even when things were bad there was always something I enjoyed. Kicking a ball round on a bit of wasteland or running errands to earn pennies.'

'Where's your sister now?'

He fiddled with a button on his coat.

'Australia. One of those assisted voyages.'

The authorities paid for some kids to go out to the Colonies for better lives.

'They wouldn't take me, said I was too old or too young or not a girl or something.' There was a bitterness in his voice.

'So you're a proper orphan, then? Just like in the books.'

'A proper orphan,' he repeated. He pulled something out of his pocket. I peered at it in the dark. A small bottle. He opened it and took a quick nip, wiping the rim on his sleeve. 'Here.'

'What is it?'

'Brandy.'

I'd heard people complain that spirits were becoming impossible to get hold of. He must have read my mind. 'Found it in a bomb site.'

'Isn't that . . .?' I took the bottle from him, not certain I wanted to try it. The fumes made my eyes water.

'Looting?' He shrugged. I supposed I'd become a looter, too, technically, as I'd taken that dead rose. And would have pinched a pencil or a piece of soap if I'd found them.

I raised the bottle to my lips and let a very small amount trickle through my lips. Forcing myself not to spit it out I swallowed it and coughed. Paul Gabriel laughed.

'Bit strong for you.'

'No.' I handed it back. 'It's good.' I could feel the brandy burning through my chest. Why did people drink this stuff? I'd never even liked the smell of it when added to a Christmas pudding and set alight.

Paul's sharp ears must have picked up something I couldn't hear because he turned his head towards the blacked-out window. 'Jerry's gone.'

'The all-clear hasn't sounded yet.'

'It will.' He stuffed the brandy bottle and the rose inside his jacket, scooped up the cat and stood. 'C'mon, Rachel. Time you went back to the shelter.'

I hadn't mentioned the painting I'd found.

10

Mrs H and I sat on chairs beside Mum's bed. Mum's face had faded to the colour of the distempered hospital walls. She'd had the operation two days ago and they'd finally let me see her.

'They think they got it all,' she told us. 'They're confident.'

I wasn't. I wished Mum was in one of those clinics in Switzerland or America I'd read about, with mountain scenery and no bombs. But how could any doctors, Swiss or otherwise, be sure they'd scooped out all the angry little cancer cells? I pictured them like enemy soldiers, plundering my mother's body, taking all the strength from her tissues, trying to take over her whole system. But Mrs H said we were lucky: they were evacuating this ward to the country next week. Mum'd had her operation just in time.

Dad should have been here with her. Surely his essential work allowed for compassionate leave? Whenever I'd asked Mum why he couldn't come she mumbled something about desperate times requiring sacrifices. She didn't like me talking about Dad, I could tell. I knew his job was secret but I was discreet. For God's sake, I was hardly likely to go blabbing on about what my father was doing for the war effort, was I?

The nurse on duty this afternoon seemed to have something against us. She gave Mum her medicine and plumped up the pillows so she could sit up, but she didn't smile or reply to Mrs H's polite compliments about the shining surfaces of the ward. I saw her laughing and chatting with the middle-aged lady and thin young woman in the beds across the ward, though. So it was just us she didn't like.

I wished again that my father were here to jolly her out of her ill temper.

'Tell me where Dad works,' I begged Mum again. 'I'll find a telephone number and leave a message for him.'

'Darling, there's no need. I'm fine.'

'He should be here with you.'

'But you're both doing such a good job.' She tried to smile but her eyes gave her away. The nurse returned in a crackle of hospital starch.

'Visiting time is over.'

I looked at my watch. Still five minutes to go.

'Your mother needs her rest.' The nurse was almost growling like an Alsatian dog.

'Just a little bit longer, Nurse, please,' Mum implored.

I refused to stand, even though the nurse was now glowering at me and trying to push a little trolley laden with syringes, medicines and enamel bowls up to Mum's bed. 'I want him to be with you. He must be able to visit.'

'Well, it's not very likely, is it?' The nurse folded her arms.

Mrs H cleared her throat, as though warning her off.

'He'd get compassionate leave, wouldn't he?' I begged Mum. 'Even if it was a just a few days.'

Mum and Mrs H looked at one another.

'Compassionate leave from an internment camp?' Behind me the nurse laughed, a scornful, nasty laugh. 'I don't think so. Traitors like Professor Pearse belong behind barbed wire.'

11

Fury like I'd never known before propelled me out of the chair and at the nurse. I collided with the trolley, sending the contents crashing down to the lino floor. Even in the midst of my anger I could see the other patients in the ward nearly jumping out of bed in shock. Before I could reach the nurse to scratch her eyes out Mrs H rose up, grabbed the end of my cardigan and pulled me back. 'No, Rachel.'

The matron appeared from her office at the end of the ward, like an angry white goddess, and hauled the nurse and me off to her office. I could hardly explain what had happened. I felt like an incendiary, hissing and about to ignite. Matron didn't say much. She probably realised I wasn't in a mood to listen.

'I'm going to have to take one of my nurses off the ward to re-sterilise those scissors and syringes, something I can ill afford to do at a time like this. Lucky for you none of those medicine bottles broke, young lady.'

'I'm sorry.' I counted upwards in seventeens very quickly and felt my rage subside. 'But she's telling lies about my father.'

'I'm certainly not, Matron!' the nurse broke in. 'Professor Gregory Pearse's arrest was reported in *The Times*. He's a Fascist. The report said he had a wife and daughter living near his old university in Bloomsbury. And our patient is Mrs Gregory Pearse, living in Fulton Street, less than half a mile from the university.' She looked at me, contempt written all over her horrid puffy face. 'I'm right, aren't I?'

'He's no Fascist,' I started to say. But then I remembered the days immediately after Dad had left on what Mum had called his government work. She'd packed me off to stay with a distant cousin in the New Forest. We'd spent a quiet time walking and cycling and I hadn't seen any newspapers for about a week. When I'd finally returned, Mum was packing up our things and advertising our house for let. What had been going on while I was away? Had the police come for Dad?

'I'll pay for anything I broke,' I said, scratching the back of my hand.

Matron stared at me through her frosty blue eyes. 'That won't be necessary, Miss Pearse. But I'd like you to go back to the ward and say goodnight quietly to your mother, so she can settle down calmly.' She turned her gaze to the nurse. 'And you and I need five minutes together, Nurse Wilkins.'

'I don't know what got into me,' I whispered to Mum when I went back to her. 'I'm so sorry I upset you.' My voice gave a little tremble. 'But I couldn't have her telling lies about Dad.' The thought of that nurse still made me want to throw things out of the window.

Mum's face was ashen with fatigue.

'Darling.' She squeezed my fingers. 'Try not to worry. It's not as bad as it sounds.'

'So Dad really is in an internment camp?' I shuddered. 'Why?'

'They claim he joined some Fascist group back in the early thirties.'

'What?' My father, wearing silly black shirts and marching and shouting?

She closed her eyes. I felt sorry, keeping her talking when she was so tired, but I needed to know.

'Why would they even think such a thing?'

'The story is he went on marches, protesting about cheap labour in the East depriving British workers of jobs.'

'When?'

'Some years before the war started. When you were little.'

I tried and tried to remember Dad doing anything like this. He'd travelled for his job, it was true. But only to visit laboratories and factories. Or so he'd said.

'What about . . .' I swallowed. 'All the Jewish stuff?' I couldn't help sneaking a glance at Mrs H, waiting patiently for me at the door.

'He never had time for that kind of rubbish.' Mum seemed to find some strength and pulled herself up. 'Your father's no Nazi,' she said, her eyes burning bright. 'I can promise you that, Rachel. He's a clever and patriotic Englishman who wants to stop Hitler and wants to use his knowledge to help. This whole thing is . . . a bit of a mistake.' She looked down at her thin hands.

But how could it be a *mistake* if the authorities thought him so dangerous he had to be sent to a camp?

'Where is he?'

'The Isle of Man.'

That little island between Britain and Ireland. I couldn't think of anything more to say. I kissed her goodbye and told her I'd bring her a fresh nightdress in the morning.

All the same, it seemed strange that a Jewish person like Mrs H didn't mind being friends with Mum and me. She told me on the way home that my dad and her husband were held within half a mile of one another. Mr H had been sent there after Dunkirk when every German male – even a Jewish one – was suddenly a potential enemy.

'Only a month ago your father lectured the inmates at the camp on rubber molecules and how they changed when heated. My Ernst went to that lecture, even though he's no scientist. The prisoners try and keep themselves intellectually stimulated, to make the best of the situation. Ernst doesn't believe your father's a Nazi either, Rachel.'

I just couldn't understand any of it, it was so bizarre. That's why Mum always read Dad's letters aloud to me and burned them as soon as she had done so – the camp address must have been stamped on the paper. That's why he never ever telephoned us and couldn't get leave to visit his wife, not even when she was so ill with cancer. My father, formerly an eminent scientist, was now a political prisoner along with a lot of idiots who thought that black uniforms and jackboots were the answer.

I tried to make all the facts add up, to turn it into an equation I could solve. But the two givens – my loving, sensible father, and the horrible kind of people who joined organisations like that – just didn't seem to belong together. So there had to be some kind of mistake, just as Mum said.

But surely Mum and Dad would have fought the internment if they'd believed a mistake had been made? The authorities wouldn't send a useful scientist into captivity for no good reason. And why hadn't Mum found a lawyer or written to their MP to ask for help? Mum was protecting me. Not telling me all of it. The cold, heavy stone that weighed down my stomach when I thought of my fragmented family seemed to have grown to the size of a boulder.

Mrs H said they'd probably let Dad out at some point.

Just thinking about my father as a Fascist made me want to scratch the inflamed patches on my skin and make them bleed. The blood-letting would have given me some relief, but I managed to stop myself, knowing it would only make Mrs H and Mum more anxious and do no good.

As if there hadn't been enough drama this afternoon, we reached home to find a woman waiting for us in the entrance hall. Something about her sensible brown lace-up brogues and milk-bottle spectacles told me she was from the authorities. This time it was the education board. She wanted to know why I wasn't in school.

'I'm nearly fifteen,' I said. 'I don't have to go any more.' I probably sounded rude and sullen. I was still recovering from the revelations.

'You may be school-leaving age, Rachel, but according to our records you were staying on to study for your School Certificate.'

School Certificate's the bit of paper you need if you want to go on to university or do more than work on the cash register at Boots or put in curlers at a hairdresser's.

Mrs H took the woman upstairs and made her some tea. She explained about my old school being bombed, telling her that my mother was still exploring various alternative educational possibilities. A nice way of putting it.

'I'm in the library for hours most days,' I added, hoping to impress. 'I spend hours on mathematics. And I've just this week learned the map of Brazil off by heart.'

The Education Board woman – Miss Hollis was her name – frowned. 'Education is more than just learning facts and figures, Rachel. It's about equipping you for the future, preparing you to help rebuild this country after the war.'

I knew what Miss Hollis meant, but didn't want to admit it.

'Maths is one of the most important subjects you can study.' I sounded defensive, surly almost.

'Of course it is! But you're a clever girl, Rachel, you need to study everything you can.'

Dad's famed cleverness hadn't got him very far, had it?

'*Ich liebe dich!*' Perseus told her.

'*Danke*,' she replied. '*Ich liebe dich auch.* I love you too.'

I couldn't help warming to Miss Hollis a little then. I wondered what she'd say if I told her I was studying at the University of the Blitz with someone who knew the things that mattered. Where to shelter when raids grew fierce. How to get hold of scarce luxuries. How to *survive*.

Mrs H looked at her watch. 'We really should prepare supper, Rachel. That alert will go very soon.'

'I must be on my way, too.' Our visitor rose, brushing at the creases in her thick flannel skirt and telling us not to bother seeing her out. 'I'll write a report saying I'm perfectly satisfied that your education isn't suffering, Rachel. But this can only be a temporary measure. You need to be back at school.'

'There you are.' Mrs H smiled at me when Miss Hollis had left. 'That wasn't so bad, was it? She understands.'

'I wish I did.' I could have kicked myself for sounding so forlorn, like a little kid. Mrs H walked to me and put her arms around me. I breathed in her scent.

'Try not to worry about your parents. This difficult time will pass more easily if you can think positively.'

I knew of one thing I could do, one person who could help me do this. I ate my dried-egg omelette in silence, wondering how I could slip away to see him. Mrs H tutted.

'Look at the state of this kitchen.' I looked. It seemed as immaculate as ever, the drying-up cloth folded over the oven handle, the lino gleaming. 'I'd better clean it before we go to the shelter.'

'I'll help.'

'*Nein.* You go on ahead, Rachel. Reserve our usual place.'

Perhaps she needed time alone, time to soothe herself. Having someone my age around all the time must be wearisome for her.

'All right.'

The gods were shining on me because when I reached the Tube station alone Paul Gabriel was waiting for me. My heart thumped at the sight of the skinny frame in the sharply cut black overcoat. He nodded a greeting and thrust a small bottle into my hands.

'Gotta go, busy night.' This is for your mum. Morphine. I've heard rumours about shortages in hospitals.'

I was still thanking him when he looked over my shoulder and frowned, the way he had the second time we'd met.

'God damn it.' And he was off, running like a whippet.

Coming round the corner with his ugly dog was the man in green tweed I'd seen by the pub.

His eyes narrowed as he spotted Paul but he didn't attempt to pursue him – he wouldn't have had a prayer against Paul's long legs. He stood for a moment as though considering his options before walking on. I went a few steps down the Tube stairs, muttering an apology to those I jostled. Hidden from the street I peered up through the railings to see where he was going. Heading north, apparently. I thought of the Blue Lion in Windmill Street.

The alert sounded. I ran back up the steps against the flood of people descending to the platform and looked down the street. The man and dog were already crossing Tottenham Court Road. I followed, careful not to come too close. They turned into Windmill Street and halted at the pub door. I stooped behind a letter box. The man pushed open the door and scanned the interior. Then he slammed the door and set off again, dragging the dog after him. Something in that pub had put the wind up him all right.

Really I should have been heading straight back to the shelter. The anti-aircraft had already started firing. How much longer would it take Mrs H to polish her kitchen to a sheen? She'd be coming down to that platform looking for me at our usual space by the fire bucket. But I really needed to see who was in that pub.

I left my hiding place and walked up to the begrimed windows to peer in. I couldn't see Paul

Gabriel, but there was someone I knew paying for a drink at the bar: Inspector Blake. He took his drink into the snug and sat down, back facing the door.

I found myself opening the pub door. The Blue Lion was full tonight. Nobody here seemed worried about the raid – they all carried on smoking and drinking the watery beer and talking about racing results. I eased myself inside, smelling the pub's particular blend of odours, and found myself a seat next to two stout men who were discussing greyhounds. I was near enough to Inspector Blake to make out some of what he was saying to an elderly man so smartly dressed that he could only be a foreigner.

I didn't know what was possessing me to do this. But nobody paid me any attention.

'You mean Francis O'Leary?' the elderly man asked.

'I'm not going to comment on individual names.'

I moved a fraction closer to the snug.

'It'll be Francis you want.' The foreign man sounded as though he came from Eastern Europe.

'Tell me about him,' Inspector Blake said.

'You're the policeman. What do you know?'

'A Catholic from Northern Ireland. Hates Britain.'

I knew about Northern Ireland. Some of them, the Catholics, hadn't wanted to stay British when the rest of Ireland had broken away to become independent.

'That's where you're wrong.' The old man seemed to be gloating. 'I first met him myself coming out of a cricket match at Lord's. The man loves – loved – this country, but he was never allowed to belong here.'

'Wrong religion?'

'He only had to open his mouth and it was very clear that everything about him was wrong: accent, religion and class.'

Dad always said that the class system was a terrible trap for most British people.

'So Francis turned to Dublin?'

'Dublin, Moscow, Berlin.'

'Moscow? Really?' Inspector Blake sounded surprised.

'Francis had his Bolshevik fantasies.' The old man laughed.

I knew the Bolsheviks were Russian revolutionaries. They'd always sounded rather exciting and romantic. But Dad told me that he'd heard things about what went on in Russia these days. Bad things. Cruel things.

A glass clinked on the table. 'I'm surprised you didn't pick him up years ago.'

'Hard to pin anything on him. His minions do the dirty work.' A chair squeaked as Inspector

Blake stood. 'But we've received some interesting intelligence from . . .' His last words were muffled as he put on his overcoat and trilby. I picked up a discarded *Evening News* and stuck my head into it. I couldn't help glancing at part of a news story about a bomb shattering the glass ceiling of a nightclub and killing lots of people who were dancing there.

'So you'll be in touch, sir,' Inspector Blake said, 'if you hear anything? Our contact thinks the target has visited the chosen location.'

A sigh. 'You mean Paul Gabriel?'

I nearly dropped the newspaper.

'I know you still harbour sentimental views about that boy.'

'I've known worse lads, Inspector,' the old man said. 'Where I came from, pushing elderly Jews over balconies was a popular pastime for the local youths.' I peered over the top of the newspaper.

'Nobody thinks Gabriel's like that. He's just been led astray.' The inspector sounded as though he was trying to soothe the old man. 'But how can we stop him from getting into worse trouble if we can't get hold of him? And O'Leary. He's the key.'

'All right.' His companion sounded weary. 'I'll keep in touch.' They started to walk through the pub. 'Your "location" is Lord Street, isn't it? That boarded-up house – can't remember which number it is. There's a ginger cat that hangs around outside.'

The inspector glanced around, as though worried someone might be listening in. I raised the newspaper again.

'You're observant.'

'Where I grew up people learned to keep their eyes open. Won't Paul Gabriel wonder why on earth his contact suddenly wants to tip him off about a valuable piece of art?'

'The contact is the type who has been out and about a lot. They often pass on bits of information of this kind.'

'Hmm. Do they now? Good evening to you.'

I kept my head in the newspaper, staring at the article about the nightclub bombing, and waited, counting to one hundred very slowly before making my own exit.

Bombs crumped nearby. Somewhere this side of Regent's Park, I estimated. As I ran back to the shelter, dodging the irate warden, snatches of overheard conversation blew through my mind. *Ginger cat. Paul Gabriel. O'Leary.*

I spotted Mrs H marching along towards the Tube and broke into a faster sprint to ensure I was ahead of her going down to the platform.

12

'I've been looking for you. It's important.' I'd been watching out for him for the last two days and here was Paul Gabriel at last, appearing in the fitful afternoon sun like something conjured up by a magician, striding out among the tired housewives scouring the shops in search of food.

He leaned against the grocer's window, obscuring the display of Bird's Custard Powder and boxes of dried eggs, and narrowed his eyes at me. I was wearing a pleated skirt that barely skimmed my knees, a pair of socks rolled down to my ankles, and an old beret of Mum's. I'd decided to go for the art-student look, rather than bother with darned stockings. The skin on my legs seemed to be a little less pink today and I didn't feel so bad about exposing it.

'The police were talking about you.'

'Tell me something new.'

'Inspector Blake was in the Blue Lion with this funny old foreign man.'

Paul Gabriel stood up straight. 'Foreign man?'

'Old. Very smartly dressed.'

'Damn.' He frowned. 'I hadn't realised they'd tracked him down.' I expected he'd go straight on the run, the way criminals do in the pictures, but he showed no signs of making a bolt for it. 'Feel like coming back to the house with me?'

'To Lord Street?' Already the place was building up an image in my mind almost like Fagin's den in *Oliver Twist*. 'But aren't you worried about going there? They know all about it.'

'Thought they might.' His eyes still challenged me. 'Coming?'

I thought of all the excuses I could give: Mrs H had asked me to track down some white fish to fry for supper, I hadn't done much studying today, I needed to iron a freshly washed nightdress for Mum. But my feet seemed to follow Paul Gabriel before I'd given them my consent.

We walked past the fishmonger with his display of smelly snoek fish from South Africa, and past the butcher with his grey sausages and trays of animal organs that not even Mrs H could find ways of cooking, and the greengrocer with his hairy carrots and muddy-leaved cabbages.

In silence we strolled up Mortimer Street, cutting alongside the Middlesex Hospital, where

Mum lay in bed imagining me doing something completely innocent, like all those errands. Nurses bustled along the road on their way to another shift of blood-stained bodies. Doctors smoked outside on the street, eyes blank, faces pale from all the long shifts, soaking up the daylight.

When we reached Lord Street the ginger cat was on the windowsill. Seeing us, he miaowed.

'Someone must be feeding him.' I glanced over my shoulder as though whoever it was might be watching us. Meanwhile Paul Gabriel's strong hands had stripped the boards away from the door again. It opened without a squeak.

We walked down the corridor and through to the pantry. I half expected Inspector Blake to jump out and arrest us for looting. Paul Gabriel removed his torch from his pocket and shone it towards the wrapped-up painting. So he *had* known it was down here. Of course he had. He undid the string and pulled the painting out of its canvas covering so that he could run the torch beam over the girl. Contradicting blackout regulation, the torch was untaped. The bright yellow ray picked out the girl's pearl buttons and the strands of bronze in her hair. And the milk-white, spotless hands.

'Looks like you, doesn't she?' Gabriel focused his torch on her face. 'Same eyes. Her hair's a bit darker, though.'

I wasn't used to people commenting on my appearance. In our family it wasn't thought quite the thing. My parents only ever said that I looked smart, or in need of a haircut or new coat.

'I suppose she does.' I took a step closer and traced the hem of her dress. 'Or rather, I look like her. Except for my bloody skin.' The swearword dropped out naturally. Mum would have killed me.

'Let me have a look at your hands.'

I opened my mouth to protest but something stopped me. Why not? There was something about this boy which meant I could be open with him, that I could uncover myself. I removed my gloves.

He took my hands in his. 'It's getting better.'

I hadn't been scratching the dry skin as often in the last few days. The scaly bit on my cheek had almost vanished. 'I don't know why.'

'Perhaps it's because you like the danger, Rachel. All this,' he nodded in the direction of the street, 'stops you worrying so much about the rest of your life.'

Perhaps he was right. Perhaps the physical danger was a kind of distraction: welcome relief from what really terrified me, that fear that Mum would die and Dad would never come back and I'd be left alone. I took a deep breath. I'd never admitted to myself before how much this prospect terrified me. Why couldn't everything go back to the way it had been before the war, with me safe and treasured, the only child of two kind parents? But I knew that, even without Hitler, I could never return to being that girl again. She was gone, along with Bounder and Cadbury's Dairy Milk on a Saturday morning.

I didn't know what to say to Paul Gabriel. What was passing through my mind didn't seem to have words to express it. I looked back at the girl in the painting. He kept holding my hands.

'She looks valuable. Perhaps she's an Old Master or something. Inspector Blake was talking about a man called O'Leary, the green tweed man. Is he interested in this picture?' *Are you going to steal it for him?* I wanted to ask.

He dropped my hands. 'They were talking about O'Leary, were they?' He seemed suddenly ill at ease.

'The inspector wanted to know all about him.' I glanced over my shoulder, feeling nervous again. 'You don't think they could be waiting outside for us, do you?'

'Not today.'

'Why not today?'

He blinked and seemed to come back into the present.

'They'll still be sniffing round Piccadilly. You know that big bomb last night, the one that went through the glass ceiling in the nightclub – that's where they'll be.'

I remembered the story about the bomb I'd glanced at in the *Evening News*.

'Plenty of pickings there. The coppers will be taking an interest.'

I'd seen those girls going off to a nightclub, dolled up in their evening dresses and jewellery, some of them only a couple of years older than me. I couldn't think of anything to say. Yet Paul sounded almost unbothered by the deaths.

He turned back to the painting.

'I don't know much about art but I do know I like her.' His fingers traced the brocade on the hem of the girl's dress. 'Why do you think she's bothered by her reflection in the mirror?'

It was a relief to move away from the subject of the bombed nightclub. 'Can't be because she's worried about her looks,' he said.

I thought I knew how the girl felt. Unsure of herself as a person, worried she wasn't up to whatever life was going to throw at her. Worried there might be something in her reflection that she'd missed.

'It's bait.' He started to wrap the painting up again. 'They want me to go for it.'

I shivered.

He looked at me. 'You all right?'

'I don't like this. They're out to get you.'

'They can try.' He didn't look worried. He scrutinised me more closely. 'It's not just your mum, is it, that's on your mind? It's something else.'

'Her temperature's down. They're pleased with how the operation went.'

'So what is it?'

I decided to tell him about my father, the supposed traitor. I still wasn't sure how I felt about him. I think I was veering towards believing there must be truth in what the nurse had said. Paul Gabriel wasn't exactly in a position to come over all disapproving, was he? The words came tumbling out. When I'd finished he didn't speak for a second or two.

'They'll probably let him out soon,' he said at last. 'They'll want him to help the war effort, a clever man like that.'

'It's the shock.'

'Shock?'

'Finding out that he was ever involved in that kind of thing.' I realised I was now admitting I thought the authorities must have had some grounds for imprisoning Dad. Former sympathies. Rash words. I couldn't remember these things myself but perhaps he'd been careful in front of me.

Paul gave a dismissive wave. 'Is that what you mean by a shock? Don't sound that serious to me.' He pulled the brandy bottle out of his pocket and took a sip, wiping the rim before offering it to me. 'I've met some of the Blackshirts who used to march through the East End. Your dad don't sound like them.'

I took a small swig. The brandy seared me again but my body was ready for it this time and I didn't cough. 'Dad had this map on his study wall and he was plotting the German advance on Dunkirk. Promising us they wouldn't win in the end. He said the Nazis were barbarians.'

'Well, then.' He took the brandy back from me. 'I should mix it with something to make it easier for you to drink.'

I could feel the brandy coursing through my veins. Perhaps that was why people took it, to experience this softening sensation as it warmed you.

'It helps,' Paul said. 'Takes the edge off your feelings. Sometimes it's what we need.'

Strange how this creature of the streets could make me feel better about things than anyone else, even kind Mrs H, could. He moved closer and touched my lips with his finger. The finger was warm and comforting as it moved across my cheek.

'You're a stunner,' he said. 'I never met a girl like you before.' His finger traced the outline of my mouth. I felt hot and cold, wanting to step away from him, but wanting to go closer, too.

'I'm nothing special.' And I really wasn't. Or except when I was with him.

The alert screamed. I stepped back from him. 'I've got to go.'

'Why? You're not scared of them, are you?'

It was Paul I was scared of. Not scared, exactly. I couldn't exactly describe how he made me felt. What had happened this afternoon made me feel as though someone had tipped out all the emotions in me like buttons from a jar, leaving them exposed in a pile on the floor. I needed to be alone. I needed some mathematics to calm me down.

'Liar,' he taunted.

'I'm not.'

'Prove it.'

I stared at him. He met my gaze with those strange green eyes of his. Then he shook his head. 'Nah. Forget it.'

'What?'

'You're a nice little middle-class girl, Rachel. You belong in nice middle-class areas with nice middle-class people.'

'They've all been bombed out,' I said. 'Haven't you heard? And I'm not some prim-and-proper person.'

'Prove it.'

'How?' I had a sudden cold sensation inside me. 'Do you want me to steal something else?'

He shrugged. 'You could do. Something valuable, mind.'

'The painting?' I tried to imagine myself smuggling it out under my coat and failed.

He shook his head. 'Too heavy for you. Find me a cigarette case or a necklace or something.'

I felt cold. He was still studying me.

'You haven't got much bottle, have you?' He shook his head.

'Ask me to do something else.'

'What?'

'I don't know.' Shame and misery flooded me. He was right. I would never belong to the streets the way Paul Gabriel did. I'd be an outsider here, just as I had been at all those schools. Those girls I'd despised because they went with soldiers behind blasted-out walls, they'd despised me for being so po-faced, so proper. And I was.

He let go of me, his attention already shifting away from me. 'Come to the pub tomorrow. We'll stay away from this house from now on. Something's not right here.'

13

I drank my breakfast cup of tea, wrinkling my nose at the sour taste. Mrs H had forgotten to put her milk out on the windowsill last night and it had turned. She wouldn't waste it, though. Mrs H knew how to make curd cheese and something called yoghurt from soured milk. The yoghurt looked like cream but tasted sharp. People in Europe swore by it, apparently. I'd come to like it, too.

I poured myself another cup of tea and drank it black, looking all the while at the painting Mr and Mrs H had brought with them from Berlin. It was a woman's face, but you saw the back of her head and each side all at the same time. Mrs H said it was Cubist and Hitler hated paintings like this, calling them decadent.

At first I'd had a sneaking sympathy for his assessment – I couldn't work the picture out at all and thought I could have done something similar myself. Aged eight. But as I'd sat at this table every morning over breakfast and examined the Cubist woman I'd started to see the point of her. There were bits and pieces of her depicted from all angles, but they were well drawn, I had to admit. Her right profile showed her with serene eyes and a half-smile. But the left showed her eyebrows lowered and the hint of a frown. Her hair seemed neat and sleek from the front but the back view showed ruffled curls, as though she'd been running her fingers through her hair. Which side of herself did she really want to show to the world? Perhaps we were all a little bit like that. There was Mrs H, being so cheerful and practical when she must privately be so worried. There was Mum, trying to cling on to her motherly duties to her thankless child while she was in anguish about her cancer. Paul Gabriel, seemingly so unbothered by bombs and the police, yet perhaps more wary than he wanted me to realise.

The library didn't appeal to me this morning. I felt like doing something practical to stop me thinking about Paul Gabriel. 'I might give our flat a good clean,' I said.

'Good idea.' Mrs H liked clean houses. Mum said that was typically German. 'I'll lend you my feather duster so you can give your picture rails a good going-over. So much dust these days from the vibrations.' Mrs H worried that the vibrations would do us some internal injury. As she handed me the feather duster she smiled at my hands. 'Your skin is getting better now, Rachel. Much less red.'

I touched my cheek and found it too felt softer. 'I haven't used the cream for days now.'

'Perhaps you feel a little easier about things.'

'Perhaps.' But I thought again about Paul Gabriel's theory about my response to danger healing my body.

I unlocked our front door. Already the flat had taken on the empty feel that places acquire when they're left unoccupied. It had only been a week since Mum had gone into hospital and I'd moved in with Mrs H.

I wrapped Mum's gingham apron round my skirt and started on the living room. The silver photograph frames needed polishing. I picked up a picture of the three of us. No, four. Bounder sat in my lap, ears pricked. I hoped the elderly couple in the country who'd taken him in were giving him lots of long walks. I was wearing shorts and an Aertex shirt and my uncovered arms and legs looked clear and healthy. I tried to remember when the eczema had first flared up. It must have been around the time Dad had left and I'd been sent off to stay with Mum's school-friend. Thinking about those days made me want to scratch behind my knees but I satisfied the urge by attacking the silver frame with the polish and cloth instead, rubbing it until my wrist ached and the metal gleamed.

I threw away the dahlias Mum had left in a vase before she went into hospital. Normally she'd have done it herself. She must have been too weak. Or perhaps she'd hoped she might really be back here before they were dead. I ran the carpet sweeper over the rugs and plumped up the saggy cushions on the sofa. Dust had fallen everywhere; I had to use three dusters. I moved to the other rooms, tidying, dusting, sweeping, banging rugs out of windows. In Mum's room I found her sewing basket, lid open, threads of cotton tangled round one another. I sat on the bed and untangled them, wrapping each thread neatly round its bobbin, wishing I could so neatly unwrap and untangle my own family's threads and return us to order. But it was impossible. My father's treachery – it must be treachery, surely? Mum's cancer, these were strings that could not be pulled straight and re-wound. Once a thread is frayed it can never be made good again. It has to be cut.

I replaced the sewing basket in the wardrobe and turned my attention to the windows. I polished the glass panes with vinegar and news-paper until they shone between the tapes we'd criss-crossed over them to prevent them from shattering.

The results of all this domesticity were oddly pleasing, but had worn me out. I flopped down in Mum's armchair and picked up one of her old magazines. It was all about fashionable dresses and fashionable people. The clothes in the photographs were gorgeous, but who could find dresses and suits like these in London nowadays? All those elegant females in their satin evening gowns were probably digging up potatoes or driving ambulances. Or lying dead with their peaches-and-cream complexions ripped by glass. I shuddered and put down the magazine.

Last night had been noisy, the rumble of explosions and guns preventing sleep, even down there on the platform. I'd sat there telling myself off for having been such a fool with Paul Gabriel in the Lord Street house. A boy like that would take advantage. But another voice, deeper inside me, told me Paul wasn't like that.

Then the raid had finished and we'd come back to Mrs H's but still I couldn't sleep, the clanging of ambulance bells heading towards the Middlesex Hospital keeping me alert. I'd wondered about the wounded people in the ambulances, who they were and who was worrying about them.

After lunch I'd go and visit Mum, braving that nurse.

* * *

I handed over the bottle of morphine while Mrs H was arranging the asters we'd bought in a vase. They weren't anything special – cut flowers were rare these days. 'Take this in case they run out.'

Confusion made my mother look almost like a little girl. 'What is it, darling?'

'Morphine. For the pain.'

'Is this a little joke?' She was smiling but her eyes were puzzled.

'No.'

'They give me enough medicine.' She peered at the bottle. 'Where did you get this? Who gave it to you?'

'There we are.' Mrs H finished arranging the flowers on the bedside cabinet and turned to us, providing a distraction. 'Have they dressed your wound again today?' She was studying Mum, lips slightly pursed.

'Yes. The nurse said it looked a little puffy.' The two women exchanged meaningful looks. I knew what they were worrying about: infection. If only we could get hold of some of that wonder drug, penicillin, or something. Perhaps Paul Gabriel . . . But no, bad idea.

Mum's cheeks were very pink against the paleness of the rest of her face, yet the ward was hardly overheated: Matron was obviously a fresh-air fanatic and windows were left open night and day. Mrs H went to speak to the nurse. Mum pulled the small bottle of morphine out from under the sheet where she'd hidden it.

'Take this home and we'll talk about it when I'm well.' I tried to work out from her face whether she was cross or just concerned. Any moment now she'd ask who had given it to me. Fortunately the bell rang for the end of visiting time. Mum's face softened as she looked at me. 'I like your new outfit,' she said.

I'd forgotten to put on my stockings and still wore my art-student rolled-down socks and the beret. Dressing like this had become a habit.

'But Rachel, the lipstick would look better if you blotted it on a piece of tissue paper first.'

Mum sank back on her pillows, a gleam of amusement brightening her face.

'I need to go to the library before it closes,' I told Mrs H as we left the hospital. 'I won't be long.' I wanted to return the morphine to Paul Gabriel. No, I simply wanted to see him. I didn't even feel I needed an excuse any more, that's how far gone I was. That's how much I wanted to feel his kisses on my skin, his hands stroking my hair, his voice. The gas mask bumped against my hip as I ran, covering the short distance to Windmill Street in what seemed like seconds. Too early for the pub to be open yet, but I'd wait.

I hung around for ten minutes, trying not to scratch my hands or look as though I were waiting for someone, but there was no sign of the slight, sharp-coated figure. Of course, he hadn't given me an exact time at which he might appear. I walked back to the pub window and looked in again, in case he'd sneaked inside illicitly. I'd heard some landlords weren't too bothered about keeping to licensing hours. No sign of him.

I began to walk towards Lord Street, knowing that this was exactly what Paul Gabriel had told me not to do, but feeling alarmed, sure something had happened to him.

The house appeared as it usually did, except that there was no sign of the ginger cat. I looked behind me once and then ran down the steps to the basement. The boards on the door had been removed and the door swung open to my touch. I crept inside, not daring to call out.

It was dark enough now to need a light. I reached for the torch I always kept in my pocket and tiptoed down the tiled corridor towards the pantry. No sign of him. My feet found the bottom of the stairs up to the ground floor. I'd just reached the drawing room when a figure took form in the shadows and grabbed me. I heard my torch crash on the wooden floorboards.

'Don't scream,' said Paul Gabriel.

My heart was pounding. 'You scared the wits out of me.'

'I said not to come here again, didn't I?' There was an edge to his voice, a hardness. 'It's not safe.'

'You're the one who says I should embrace danger.'

'There's danger and there's O'Leary.' He flicked on his torch. The beam hit my eyes and made me turn away.

'Why does he scare you so much?' I flung out the words like a taunt.

He considered me. 'Where he goes trouble goes too.'

'So why come back here yourself?'

He shrugged. 'Wanted to see if the painting was still here. Why did you come here?'

I took the bottle of morphine out of my pocket. 'She wouldn't take it. But it was really kind of you.' He moved the beam off my face and placed the morphine in his own pocket. As the torch beam moved, it caught the little table at the top of the stairs. I frowned. Something had changed. What? The vase was still there but the dead roses had gone. I was opening my lips to tell Paul Gabriel when he put a finger to his lips.

Then I heard it, too. Some kind of thumping noise coming from downstairs in the basement.

14

The kitchen door downstairs creaked. 'Anyone in there?'

Paul Gabriel signalled that we should go upstairs to the first floor. 'It's not the police' he whispered.

'Or O'Leary?'

He shook his head and put a finger to his lips. We crept up the staircase. Paul hesitated on the landing. 'I think it's a warden. O'Leary would be quieter.' He took me across the landing and opened a door. 'In here.' The room smelled of soap and damp: the bathroom. On one wall was a door which I guessed would open into the airing cupboard. 'Quick,' Paul hissed, tugging at the handle.

The warden was walking across the ground floor hall now, his footsteps clumsy and hesitant.

He'd be wondering how many of us there were, whether we had knives. Perhaps if he saw it was just a couple of kids he'd let us go. But I knew I was deluding myself. He'd call the police. Inspector Blake would be summoned. We'd be hauled in front of the magistrates, or worse. Mum would be appalled. People would say the traitor Professor Pearse had a looter for a daughter, but what else would you expect of a family like that?

Paul's torch showed the cupboard to be small, with almost half the area taken up in wooden shelving.

'In you go.' He wrapped his arms around me. My skin tingled at his touch, despite the seriousness of the situation. Feet clomped upstairs. Paul's heart beat fast against my chest. We tightened our grip on one another, the buttons on his overcoat digging into me. A pile of towels on a low shelf behind us felt nobbly against the backs of my legs, reminding me of seaside trips, when I ran out of the cold water to throw a towel round myself.

I felt a tension beneath my ribs. I couldn't possibly be finding this amusing. But the tightness turned into a spasm and now the muscles round my mouth were twitching too. I tried to think of my old Latin teacher at school, the sour milk at breakfast, the sinister rubbery smell of my gas mask. But none of it worked. I rocked with silent laughter. I'd read some of the interesting books on Mr H's bookshelves and recalled a passage about how laughter is used in place of sexual excitement. The thought made me feel hot and cold at the same time. Was 'sexual excitement' this feeling of simultaneous terror and rapture?

The door to the bathroom creaked open. I needed to take a breath but couldn't risk it. I tried to work out the square root of two in my head. Paul put a hand over my mouth and I felt my breath cool and moisten as it condensed on his palm. I stuck the tip of my tongue out and licked the palm. He tasted sweet and salty, both at the same time. I let my hand travel up and down his back. He released one of his own hands and ran it over my neck and shoulder bone. Good bits of me to touch because the skin wasn't dry and crusty there. I stopped my sums and concentrated on my own explorations, sending my hand up to the nape of his neck to investigate, brushing his hair. It felt smooth and soft.

Something crashed to the ground in the bathroom and there was a screech, followed by a deep yell and the pounding of heavy feet out of the room.

'That cat,' muttered Paul. 'Fool must have gone and trodden on it.'

The warden lumbered downstairs, his steps growing fainter. The basement door slammed.

We stared at one another. Paul opened the airing cupboard door. 'Lucky for us it had a handle on the inside.'

Or else we'd have been stuck in there.

I stumbled out, laughter shaking me, tension washed out of me. Paul laughed too but then his face was suddenly watchful.

'That warden may go and get the police. Or board up the door again. But we've got a moment.' He clutched me to him again and I felt his sigh on my face like a warm breeze. He pulled up my chin towards him and kissed me on the lips. This time his tongue gently pushed my mouth open and entered me. I wanted to pull away, show him how shocked I was. But only for a second. The kiss seemed to wrench me out of childhood, change me from awkward, friendless Rachel Pearse into someone else, someone grown up, aware of what she wanted.

'You're so gorgeous.' He stroked my hair and ran his hand across my shoulders. His touch reminded me of the sea on my skin last time I'd swum, how it had unsettled and soothed both at the same time.

Then he pushed me away.

'Hurry! And Rachel . . .'

'What?' I wanted to pull him back towards me, push my mouth against his again.

'Take care tonight. Don't come looking for me.' He grabbed my hand and we ran downstairs to the basement.

I was unlocking the front door at home, reaching for my blackout torch, when I realised I'd dropped it in the Lord Street house.

The torch had my initials scratched on it.

15

I helped Mrs H prepare our evening meal but felt distracted, as though someone'd plugged me into a socket and charged me up with electricity. I hopped up and down, checking the blackout, fetching things from the kitchen for Mrs H, offering to wash up, to tidy, to do anything. Not that anything needed doing in this flat, which seemed to be run by a group of orderly and invisible gnomes.

Mrs H didn't seem to notice the static energy crackling around me. Or perhaps, once again, she was being tactful. Mr and Mrs H had had two sons, both of whom were now studying in American colleges. Perhaps Mrs H remembered how to handle young people as a result of bringing up Hans and Peter.

When we'd finished the meal she sat by the wireless and tapped her foot in time with the band.

'We had this dance music in Berlin before the Nazis came. *Ach*, how I loved it.'

'Did you dance with Mr Hoffman?'

'Oh, yes.' A smile softened her features. 'My Ernst is a good dancer. We'd dance until our legs felt like jelly when we were young.'

My legs had felt like jelly when Paul – I seemed to have dropped his surname now – and I had crammed into the tiny airing cupboard and we'd been so close.

The alert screamed.

'Time to go.' Mrs H sounded unbothered, as if we weren't really going down to the platform with its odours and subterranean rumblings. In the distance guns started firing. 'Come on, Rachel.'

The doorbell rang.

'Who can that be?' She shook her head.

'I'll go.' I opened the door to find Inspector Blake standing outside. 'Oh, Inspector.'

'I've timed this badly, but I need a word with you privately.' He was ashen.

'Is something wrong?' Mrs H called out from the living room.

Inspector Blake held out my torch.

'It's fine,' I called back. 'The inspector found my torch. I dropped it outside.' I took it from him, still warm from his grip.

'I don't want you to see that fellow again,' he said. The floor began to tremble slightly. Must be a swarm of bombers approaching. A big one.

'What fellow?'

'Don't play games with me, Rachel. You know I mean Paul Gabriel.'

I felt the blood draining from my face.

'It's my business to know about people like him and where they go and who they meet.'

Memories of the airing cupboard in Lord Street floated through my mind. A gun battery opened fire somewhere to the south.

'You don't know what Paul's like. You haven't given him a chance, he's not bad, he just – '

'No time for this now. Get down to the shelter and don't see that criminal again.' He nodded and walked off.

'You can't just order me around,' I told his retreating back. 'You're not my father.'

'Someone's got to keep an eye on you. Hurry up and get down on the platform,' he called up the stairs. 'I don't like the sound of this.'

I slammed the door and stood there, cheeks burning.

'Where did you leave your torch?' Mrs H asked. Fortunately she was packing her knitting into her bag as she asked. As she stuffed it in some of the stitches fell off.

'Let me.' I grabbed the needles and retrieved the dropped stitches, head turned so she couldn't see my burning cheeks. I mumbled something about getting my things from my room and we were running downstairs, the building shaking as we reached the entrance hall.

'Ah, Rachel, it's bad tonight.' Mrs H's normally calm face was taut. 'I forgot to cover Perseus!'

'Nobody'll hear him above this,' I reassured her.

'Did we lock my front door?' She hesitated on the front steps.

A resounding thump a block away made us clutch one another.

'No time to go back,' I told her.

As we turned the corner into Tottenham Court Road exploding shells and flares pierced the heavens, searchlights picking out the gigantic silver barrage balloons. It might have been a giants' fireworks night. The sky was bright like a slash of amber silk above the darkness of the streets. Up there the air would be clear, not like it was down below. London smelled like an iron left on too long.

The raid felt different tonight, more menacing, more personal, as though the planes had picked out this square mile for their dreadful work. Perhaps I was growing tired of it all, I thought as we made our way to the Tube station. Perhaps Mum had been right when she'd warned me that the excitement of the Blitz would wear off, that lack of sleep would exhaust me and play on my nerves.

Perhaps. But I still knew I wouldn't have missed the last two weeks for anything.

We had to queue just to reach the ticket office, then squash ourselves into the crowd descending the steps to the platform. The tightly packed bodies smelled of cheese and onion, overlaid with the whiff of fear. The transport police waved on laggards and told off pushers and shovers. We went down slowly, the underground reek of hot metal, wet newspapers and stale clothes rising to meet us. I felt a clamp tightening round my neck. I turned to Mrs H to tell her that I couldn't do this tonight, I'd have to go back up to the surface.

The building shuddered as though a giant hand was rocking it. Air rushed away. The stairs trembled beneath our feet, everything happening in slow motion. The white tiles on the walls turned into missiles and hurled themselves at us. Chunks of brickwork from the ceiling dropped down and the lights flickered before going out completely. People screamed. Something struck me on the temple. I felt a warm stickiness on my face and heard Mrs H call out once before the world swirled into total blackness. As I sank down, a train rumbled in below.

Was I sleeping? Or was this the afterlife: a whorl of darkness and hidden voices calling out? I drifted from shadow to shadow. At last the blackness turned to silvery grey and I knew I was awake again. Feeling a coldness in my stomach like a block of ice. Trying not to scream.

'Mrs Hoffman?' I thought I heard voices but they disappeared as I tried to make out what they were telling me.

Then nothing.

Panic like a heavy blanket suffocated me. I grabbed at numbers in my mind but they all failed me.

Eventually I must have lost consciousness for a while. I opened my eyes. An electric ringing in my ears made it hard to hear anything. I saw people lying below and above me, but no Mrs H. The ringing faded to a hum. The darkness seemed faintly lighter now, I could make out shadows where before there had been absolute blackness.

I stood up, legs trembling, stomach heaving. My forehead was stinging: I must have cut it. I picked my way up the escalator, avoiding the motionless grey shapes. No sign of her.

'Hang on, miss.' Out of the dust and ash a hand stretched towards me. An auxiliary, helping with the rescue. I grabbed at him, reassured by the warmth of his skin that he was flesh and blood, not some kind of spectre. How long had we been down here in the dark? He shone a torch in my face and the brightness hurt like a blow. 'Let's get you up.'

'You need to find Mrs Hoffman.' I waved a hand towards the escalator. 'She must still be down there.' The auxiliary muttered something to a second rescuer.

'Give me your satchel and bedding.' I hadn't realised I was still clutching them. The men pulled me up towards a rectangle of light where the blast had ripped into the station. At the top of the escalator was a void, spanned by a temporary wooden ladder. I closed my eyes, letting the rescuers guide me up and finding myself in what was left of the ticket hall, reeking of smoke and burned metal. Blanketed shapes lay in neat rows. I averted my eyes from a single shoe and a briefcase, placed neatly beside one of the motionless forms. If we'd arrived a minute later we'd have been standing right here when the bomb had landed.

So this was the Blitz. I'd mocked those who feared it but now I knew. I tried again to soothe myself by listing the divisors of my favourite perfect number, 8,128. I retrieved a few of them from the safe recesses of my memory before I gave up the effort.

An ambulance driver took me by the arm. 'C'mon, miss. Let's get you loaded up.'

'But my friend. I can't leave her – '

'They've probably already taken her to hospital. We'd pulled out some of the others before we found you.' He patted my shoulder.

'Sixty-three,' I muttered to myself, making another big effort.

Minutes later the ambulance drew up outside the Middlesex. The crew took me up to a ward and a young nurse, not the one who hated us because of Dad, thank God, examined my head and put on a dressing. Then they made me lie down. I must have dozed because when I woke it was already dawn and a yellow-grey light was oozing through the ward, revealing white-faced patients and nurses with dark shadows under their eyes.

'I'd keep you in,' said the sister when she checked my notes, 'but we haven't got enough beds. You'll do as well sitting quietly at home.' She must be assuming there was someone at home. Suppose Mrs H were dead? Mum might die, too, and then there'd never be anyone at home for me again, or not until the war ended and Dad came home. The authorities would send me to some kind of institution. I bit my lip and forced myself not to show my sense of abandonment. I couldn't show a chink. I didn't want the hospital to keep me in.

'Be careful of drowsiness and unusual vomiting,' the sister went on. The old me would have told her that any kind of vomiting was unusual for most people. But I kept my mouth shut. 'At least you're near enough to come back in if there are any complications.' She scanned the ward. 'An orderly will take you down and make arrangements for you to be driven home.'

'It's no distance at all to my flat. I'd rather walk. The fresh air – '

'Out of the question with a head injury like that.'

'I was with my neighbour, a Mrs Hoffman, when the bomb landed. Is she here too?' The sister frowned. 'Hang on, I'll check the lists.' She bustled over to the nursing station and returned with a sheet of paper. 'Eva Hoffman, female, fifty-six. Transferred to St Thomas's because we didn't have enough beds.'

'Is she badly hurt?' I thought again of 8,128 to brace myself if it was bad news.

'Concussion and a cut on one arm. They'll probably just keep her in for observation.' The sister pursed her lips. 'As we should be doing with you, really. But you do have someone at home, don't you?'

'My father.' The lie came quickly and I kept my eyes on the sister's face. I heard the rat-tat-tat of shoes on lino and heard the crackle of hospital starch. The matron from Mum's ward stood before me.

'We've got a bed free upstairs for that shrapnel operation, if you need it, Sister.' She frowned at me. 'Don't I know you, young woman?'

I kept my face neutral.

'You're Mrs Pearse's daughter.' I prayed she wouldn't tell the sister what had happened last time she'd seen me. The matron turned to the sister. 'You're keeping her in, aren't you? There's nobody at home.'

'I'll be fine,' I said.

The sister sighed. 'You should have told me you'd be going back to an empty house, Rachel. I'll ring the children's ward and see if they can help.'

The *children's* ward! Bawling toddlers and kids with measles.

I nodded meekly, letting the two of them walk off. Then I grabbed my things and legged it out of the ward, reaching the lift in three strides, but not daring to wait for it. I took the stairs two at a time even though my head was spinning. I thought I heard an angry shout behind me but I kept on going.

On the street I slowed down. My temples throbbed. Mum was going to kill me when she found out about this. Hopefully the matron would be too busy to tell her for a while. I'd visit Mum in the afternoon, slipping in when the matron wasn't looking, to reassure her I was fine. And I'd look in on Mrs H too, in St Thomas's. In the meantime I'd go home, run a bath – if the water and gas were on – and change and get something to eat. Then spend the morning in the library with paper and pencil and algebra textbook. If I passed out there someone would notice.

I reached our house and pushed open the entrance door. It wasn't locked. Inside something looked different. The light fell onto the staircase in a way it only did if Mrs H's front door was open, streaming in unbroken from her living-room window. We'd shut the door on our way to the station, but I remembered Mrs H worrying that she'd left it unlocked.

I glanced upstairs. Could there still be looters in the flat? I thought of overcoming my reluctance to see Inspector Blake and knocking on his door, but he'd be at work. I tiptoed up-stairs, straining my ears for sounds. Nothing.

Nothing? Last night Mrs H had forgotten to cover Perseus's cage so by now he ought to be whistling and calling out words of love in the language of the poet Goethe. I went inside the flat. The blackout was still down in the living room and I pulled it up. Mrs H had left the sash window open an inch at the top. She didn't like to leave a room unventilated.

Nothing seemed to have been taken. The Cubist painting was still on the wall. Probably nobody would know that it was valuable because it looked so strange. The drawers hadn't been opened. The wireless still sat on the cabinet beside the fire. I checked the sideboard and counted the silver candlesticks and bowls the Hoffmans had brought from Germany. I couldn't be sure they were all still there. Hadn't there been some teaspoons in a little box as well?

Then I walked to the uncovered birdcage stand. On the bottom lay Perseus, his neck twisted and his small black eyes dull. He must have started his German chatter at daybreak, words drifting down to the street, enraging whoever it was who'd previously complained about the budgerigar. Or encouraging a burglar to come in and have a look around the Hoffmans' flat.

I don't know how I made my way to Bedford Square Gardens from the flat. I have no memory even of crossing Tottenham Court Road. Somehow I found a bench and flopped down. I felt as though my body were full of sand and wished I could find somewhere warm, dark and safe to lie down. I closed my eyes.

A shadow fell over me.

'What happened?' Paul Gabriel pointed at my head.

'I was in the Tube when the bomb landed.'

'I heard about that.' One of his hands touched the top of my head so softly I could have missed it.

'Our neighbour was with me.'

'She was hurt?'

I nodded, staring hard at my hands, trying to think of numbers. 'But that's not it, that's not what . . . Someone got into her flat and killed her budgie. Just because it knew a few German words.'

He sat down beside me.

The pain in my head seemed to swirl up my emotions into a tornado. Rage made me sit up straight. I could feel it heating my blood, filling me with a white energy.

'But that's what people like you do, isn't it? You go into people's empty homes and take precious things. How do you think that makes them feel?'

He said nothing.

'I should have listened to Inspector Blake. I thought it didn't matter, that they were all rich people and could replace the stuff you stole. But it does matter.' I rose. 'You . . .' I searched for the word I wanted, 'defile their homes when they're already scared or sad or lonely. I don't want to see you again.'

'But Rachel – '

'Go away.' I pushed his restraining arm from me.

'I don't – ' The siren wailed. A daytime raid. We hadn't had one of those for weeks now. I was back in that escalator shaft and the bomb was falling. My stomach heaved and I tasted the bitterness of my empty stomach. The false energy that had filled me leaked away. I clutched the back of the bench. Black dots floated in front of my eyes and I flinched at the tiles flying at me. My rescue, my escape from hospital, the discovery of the dead bird, all these details had distracted me away from what had actually happened when the bomb crashed on to us. Until now. I could even smell the singed bricks, see the covered bodies in the ruined ticket office, that briefcase . . .

Paul Gabriel was taking me by the hand 'It's all right. I'll look after you, Rachel.'

'Not a shelter,' I muttered. 'Not underground again. Not today.'

Buried alive. Suffocated.

'We'll go to Lord Street.'

I blinked. 'But – '

'The coppers won't be going there in this.'

16

Even though Paul Gabriel was one of the thinnest people I'd ever known he somehow seemed the most substantial thing on the streets. While wan-faced shoppers raced to the shelters, shouting at children to hurry, he seemed almost relaxed, as though we were strolling along a seaside promenade. Despite the ever-louder drone of planes I felt myself relax, too.

'Is Lord Street really safe?' I asked. But even if it wasn't, where else could we go? I shuddered at the thought of going back to Fulton Street.

'For half an hour or so. These daytime raids don't last long. We'll sit down in the basement till it's over. I've got some business. Then I'll take you home.'

Business. He meant that wretched painting. He was going to take advantage of the raid to steal the painting before the police could spring their trap.

'You'll be safe with me,' he said. Sometimes I detected a different accent – slower and softer – beneath his quick London way of speaking.

'Paul, did you ever live in the country?' I asked, raising my voice against the din of the sirens.

His face betrayed surprise. 'How did you know?'

'Just a guess. Sometimes when you talk it sounds, I don't know, as though you lived in open space once.'

'You're like a witch, you see inside me.' But the look he gave me as he called me a witch was soft. We were nearly in Lord Street. Thank God. My legs felt shaky. Something hissed behind us. An incendiary. Paul turned and stamped on it.

'Dad was a farm labourer,' he said. 'We lived in a tied cottage on a big estate in Essex. Landlord kicked us out when Dad died of TB. So we came to Bow, where my mum grew up.'

'Do you still remember the country?'

His smile made him look younger, less a man of the streets and more of a boy.

'Blackberrying. Hares running over the meadows. Jumping off the hay bales in the barn. Oh, I remember it all right.' We were finally outside the house. I felt less heavy, as though some of Paul's electricity had fizzed through my veins.

The cat perched on the steps by the door. Paul examined the newly re-boarded door.

'They could do much better than this,' he said scornfully. 'Anyone could get in and out.' He pulled the wood away without trouble.

'What happens when we leave? They'll know we've been here.'

He patted his chest.

'I brought a hammer to bang those nails in again.' He pushed the door open and ushered me into the kitchen. The cat ran in after us, jumping on to the dresser with a single easy leap. 'We'd better make sure you leave when we do, puss,' Paul said, almost shouting now to counter the roar overhead.

We sat on the wooden kitchen chairs, scratched and homely, not like the rest of the furniture in this house. The cook would have sat down here with the rest of the staff at mealtimes. As the noises overhead grew more threatening I tried to imagine what they'd have eaten: beef stew, apple tarts, blancmanges. Perhaps scones and Victoria sandwich for tea. If I kept picturing them round this table gossiping, complaining of aching feet and munching cake I could keep the bombers at a distance.

Paul sat very still, green eyes glittering. I knew from the way he concentrated that he was reading the sounds outside, judging the position of the bombers, using those skills he'd acquired on the open streets. Had he never been scared?

Yet again he seemed to read my mind. 'The brandy's all gone now, else I'd give you some.'

Shame. I could have done with a sip to numb me.

'Some raids get to you more than others,' he went on. 'Sometimes it just seems exciting. Other times I want to do what that cat does.' He pointed at it, now wrapped up into a tight ball at the back of the dresser, hardly visible.

'Go somewhere warm and dark to hide? I suppose that's what I do with my maths.' He looked quizzical. 'Numbers are my safe place,' I explained. 'After the bomb fell on the Tube station last night I was trying to work on the divisors of 8,128.'

He looked puzzled

'It's a perfect number.' I explained what this meant. He kept his eyes on my face as I told him.

'I liked maths at school,' he said. 'Didn't get very far, though.' He reached across the table and took my hand, stroking the skin. I was glad that the scaly bits had healed. 'I steal things, you're right. And that's not good. I'd stop if I could find another way to get by.'

'That violin you had first time we met?'

'Came from a safe in a solicitor's office that blew open when the building next door took a hit. It felt like it was nobody's.'

'It still belonged to someone. Perhaps it was a musician's and when he joined up he gave it to his lawyer for safekeeping.'

Paul Gabriel's face gave nothing away.

'And the painting here, that belongs to someone, too.' I pulled my hand away.

'They didn't care much about it, then, leaving it wrapped up in a basement.'

'It's still wrong to steal it.' I sounded like a little prig but I couldn't stop myself. 'Even if it's abandoned.'

'Wrong be damned.' He stood. 'The bombers have left now. The all-clear's about to go. Go back to your flat.' He stopped and raised a hand in warning.

'What?'

'Shh.' His face was dark with some emotion. Fury? Fear? He went to the kitchen dresser and rifled through the drawers.

'What are you looking for?'

'A knife. Blast.' He kicked at the dresser. 'Nothing here.'

Footsteps rang out on the pavement above us.

The warden. He'd blow his whistle, summon police help. I thought of Inspector Blake. He was going to kill me, getting caught here again. Paul Gabriel put a finger to his lips. 'O'Leary,' he whispered. 'Don't say a word. And keep still.'

For the first time I saw fear on his face.

17

'You down there, Paulie? I think you are.' The Northern Irish accent calling down from the pavement had a mocking note to it.

We froze.

'Perhaps you're upstairs. No matter, I've got the front door key and I'm coming inside.' We heard him lumber up the steps to the front door.

Paul grabbed me. 'Out there, now.' He pushed me towards the basement door and up the steps. As I climbed them a shadow moved above us on the pavement.

'Stay where you are.'

O'Leary had his dog and a gun. His eyes were fixed on Paul Gabriel. So was the gun. I looked up and down the street for a warden, a policeman, for Inspector Blake, any kind of adult. Nobody. Everyone must be sheltering.

ELIZA GRAHAM

O'Leary and Paul were still glaring at one another. I took a step back, and O'Leary's eyes didn't move from Paul. Then I took another and another and then I was running down Lord Street, hearing O'Leary call out, expecting a bullet through my back. But even he probably didn't dare fire at a fourteen-year-old girl in broad daylight with the all-clear about to go.

I needed to find help. Or at least a weapon so Paul could defend himself. Mrs H's sharp carving knife, the one she'd used to cut the venison. I'd take that and run back to help Paul. Surely two of us could overpower him? I shuddered, remembering the dog. I hated that creature with its flabby jowls and slobbering mouth.

I covered the short distance to Fulton Street in what seemed like seconds, dodging a drunk Australian airman who wanted to buy me tea in a Lyons Corner House. I reached our house and was through the front door and halfway up the first flight of stairs when I heard the voice.

'Rachel?'

A man came out on to the landing above me. I swallowed hard. The events of the last twenty-four hours were playing tricks on me.

It couldn't be my . . .

18

... My father.

The all-clear shrieked.

Dad stood in front of me on the stairs, his arms open as wide as the world. Without thinking I flung myself up to him.

'Dad!'

I let him hug me then stood back to examine him. He was paler, thinner, older, but otherwise unchanged. Still my father.

His fingers touched the dressing on my temple. 'What happened, darling?'

'It's nothing. Just a cut.' I scratched my face where the wool in his coat had irritated my skin. I needed to get back to Paul. Now.

'I've just been at the hospital. They gave me special permission as it wasn't visiting time. Oh, Rachel, I'm so sorry you had to deal with all this by yourself.'

Perhaps you should have thought about that when you joined the Blackshirts, I wanted to say. But I didn't. He was Dad. He'd come home. I led the way upstairs into our poky little flat, the home he'd be seeing for the first time.

All the time the precious seconds ticked away. O'Leary might have shot Paul Gabriel by now. I had to get that knife. No matter how many questions for my father burned on my lips, I was needed elsewhere.

'Rachel – ' Dad broke off. Someone was coming upstairs. I stood back so that the shadows hid me from the open front door. Was it O'Leary coming for me?

'You're home at last, Professor Pearse!'

Inspector Blake. Perhaps I should tell him what was happening in Lord Street, beg him to come with me and rescue Paul. I opened my mouth to do just this. Then closed it again.

'As you see, Inspector. And it's an enormous relief.' Dad walked to Inspector Blake and shook his hand. 'Thank you for getting me out.'

I stared at the pair of them.

'We need you back in the laboratory, carrying out your experiments on rubber.' Dad specialised in developing new rubber compounds, used to make seals for industrial silos. When the war had started he told us the military wanted to use the rubber compounds for submarine hatches.

'I felt so useless in that internment camp. Everyone outside was doing useful work for the war effort except me. And Letty . . .' Dad swallowed. Letty was my mum.

'We can't afford to lose valuable scientists for long. No matter how serious the case.'

Serious. So Dad had been arrested for more than just a passing fancy for an extreme political organisation. He'd been lying to us. I wanted to get out of this room. Paul needed me. No time to explain to the inspector now. My mind was still tapping out its frantic Morse code message. *Get a weapon for Paul.* Someone needed me, Rachel Pearse.

The men sat down. I walked into the kitchen and pulled the carving knife out of the drawer, wrapping it in a drying-up cloth. Some impulse made me grab a mouldy crust of bread from the bread-bin, one I should have thought to throw out when I'd cleaned the flat. I walked to the front door.

'Just popping out for milk,' I called, hoping the sharp-eyed inspector wouldn't remember the bottle left for us on the doorstep. 'Won't be long.' I flew down the stairs and on to the street, nearly sending a pedestrian flying.

As I opened the front door to the pavement I almost tripped over the stray dog.

'Shoo!' I told him. 'Out of the way.'

I ran down the stairs and out on to the street. The stray wasn't going to let me go without him. I heard his paws padding behind me.

19

Outside the Lord Street house all was quiet. I crept up the steps to the front door and peered through the letter box. Not a sound. Had O'Leary already dragged Paul Gabriel out of the house? Or killed him? Perhaps his body lay down in the basement. Surely Paul would have kicked up a fuss, made a din, attracted the warden's attention? I walked down the basement steps on the balls of my feet, listening all the time. Now I could make out O'Leary's deep rumble and Paul's more melodic tones objecting to something.

I gave the basement door a gentle push and walked inside, leaving the door open for a hasty retreat. O'Leary hadn't locked it. Perhaps he'd thought I'd be too scared to do anything, that I'd just run to save my own skin. Well, he was wrong there. Anger was making me forget my fear.

The voices were coming from the pantry where the painting was stored. I tiptoed along the passage towards them.

My advancing shadow must have alerted the dog because it growled inside the pantry. I thought I heard an answering growl behind me. O'Leary swung round but couldn't find me in the gloom. The dog could, however. I saw that it was unleashed and was padding towards me, ears back, teeth bared, piggy eyes glinting. In a second it would growl again. Or bite me. Or both. I put my hand into my pocket and drew out the crust. I threw it over the dog's head, past the pantry door, hoping animal greed would prove more compelling than his need to confront me. He turned and trotted back towards it.

'Flynn?' O'Leary called. 'Come here.'

I only had seconds before the dog realised he'd been duped with a bit of stale bread. Then I heard another growl and looked back towards the door. My stray had followed me inside the house and stood with bared teeth, staring at the other dog gobbling down the bread.

I pulled out my knife and walked into the pantry. Paul Gabriel had been able to work round the room so that his back was to the open door. I hesitated. O'Leary had a gun. I only had a knife.

The stray barked and sprang up the passage-way towards O'Leary's dog.

O'Leary must have lost concentration for a split second. It was all Paul needed to jerk his foot up and kick the gun out of his hand.

The dogs tore back up the passageway.

'Behind you!' Paul shouted. I sprang round to see Flynn's teeth bared behind me. I flicked the knife in front of his face but he kept on coming. I'd never exactly found myself in a combat situation before, needing to hurt something living and breathing. But the expression in the dog's eyes told me I had to start learning quickly because he didn't share my scruples. So I stabbed him on his squat nose, following through with a sharp kick at his ribs. A fine line of red formed on his muzzle. He yelped and backed off and the stray snarled at him. Behind me the two men scuffled on the lino for the gun.

'Run!' Paul yelled. 'Watch the door.' I moved into the passageway, reversing back to the kitchen with the knife held out in front of Flynn. The men emerged, still fighting, Paul holding the gun but the bigger, older man clinging to it, his face contorted. In a second Paul's strength would run out and O'Leary would have the weapon again. I put my hand into my pocket, desperate to find something, anything. I found only crumbs. Then, sudden as flak, the stray was on top of Flynn, trying to grab him by the scruff. Flynn squealed. I heard his long claws scrabbling for purchase on the slippery tiles and there was a thud as the two dogs collided with O'Leary's legs. He swore and let go of Paul in an attempt to save himself from falling. And suddenly Paul was sprinting through the kitchen. He didn't have the gun. O'Leary was shouting at him to stop.

Flynn had gained control of the fight and now it was my stray who ran for the door. I waited for him to exit and slammed shut the door. The three of us sprang up the basement steps to the street. Paul grabbed my hand.

'This way.' The stray bolted in the opposite direction.

We passed house after house and I could think of nothing except getting away from that man.

Paul slowed and halted. 'We're safe now.' He was still holding my hand. I didn't want him to let go. Wherever he was going now, I wanted to go too. But I had responsibilities: Mum, Mrs H. And Dad. I needed to talk to my father.

Perhaps Paul picked up these conflicting emotions. He dropped my hand.

'Go home. Stay home. O'Leary doesn't know your name or where you live. You'll be safe if you keep your head down.' He looked back up Lord Street. 'Go on, Rachel.'

'When will I see you again?'

'I don't know. It mightn't be safe for you.' He started to walk away. 'You were a star back there. A heroine. Just like in the films. And give that dog of yours a sausage or something.'

'Oh, he's not mine,' I said.

20

It seemed as though I must have been away for ages but when I looked at my watch I saw it had only been half an hour or so. I picked up the pint of milk the milkman had left for Mrs H. in the morning and walked up to our flat, amazed that I could be doing something so ordinary so soon after all that had happened in Lord Street.

I walked in as silently as I could. 'I'm worried about the girl,' Dad said. 'Her head looks nasty.' Come to think of it, I did feel slightly queasy now. And my head was pounding. 'She shouldn't be here in London. Ah, here she is now. Hello, Rachel.'

'Sorry.' I tried to sound it. 'We'd run out of milk and I had to walk round to the dairy.'

'Was there a queue?' the inspector asked.

I nodded. He turned back to my father. 'Getting back to what you were saying about the new bomb, it sounds like pure fiction.'

'Some of the best scientists on each side think it's possible. We'd better hope our people get there first.'

'Did you hear conversations on this subject on the Isle of Man?'

'Nothing overt.'

I went into the kitchen and replaced the knife in the drawer and put on the kettle, fragments of conversation drifting through to me.

'Rachel could do with having you at home. There are all types hanging around London at the moment.'

'I'll have some leave at weekends from time to time. I'll find a cottage near the lab where the two of them can join me eventually.' A pause. 'Assuming Letty . . . well, you know.'

'She's in good hands. Her consultant's one of the best in the country, I've heard.'

The cups on the tray rattled as I took it into the living room. I was worried they'd notice but they seemed oblivious. What would the inspector say if I told him I'd been so close to his prime suspect? Dad was frowning at my hands.

'What's happened to your skin, darling?'

'It's just eczema.' Of course, I'd only started getting it after Dad had gone and he hadn't seen the patches before. He stared at me, probably sensing how much I'd grown up since he'd left. So much had happened since then. 'It's getting much better now.'

'I thought it might be another air-raid injury.' He looked relieved.

'The air raid didn't really hurt me.' I decided not to tell them about having lost consciousness in case they did something silly like take me back to the hospital, where that matron would have me incarcerated with the kiddies.

I poured the men their tea and went to find the aspirin in the bathroom cabinet. I planned on sitting quietly in my bedroom for a while by myself, perhaps working on a few equations.

Until my pulse had a change to stop racing.

21

Dad spent the evening unpacking his small suit-case. When that was done he paced our small living room, reminding me of an animal taken from the wild and put into a small cage at a zoo. At home in Putney he'd had his study and there'd been the lab to drive to if he wanted to do some research. In fact, that very same lab was only five minutes' walk away from this flat. But he wouldn't be returning to the university, he said. He'd take up this new post shortly. Then life would return to something near normal.

As far as he was concerned, perhaps. Questions burned on my lips. I made him some supper: a bit of bacon fried up with some leeks and a slice of bread. He ate it with relish. When he'd finished he put down his knife and fork.

'Rachel –'

'There's an apple, too, if you want. It was on Mrs H's fruit bowl getting soft, so I took it. She won't mind. She's very generous, she –'

'There are things I need to tell you, things you don't understand.'

'Or I could make you some cocoa. There's even a little bit of sugar to go in it.'

'I don't know what your mother told you about why I left home so suddenly?'

I stood with my back to him, fiddling with the blackout curtain. 'She told me you were doing essential work. Obviously not the truth, as I found out later.' My voice quivered.

'It's not what it seems, that's all I can say.'

The siren sounded and I jumped up with relief. 'We need to get down to the shelter.' I showed him how to roll up blankets. 'We'll just check Mrs H's door is properly locked as we go down.'

It was a relief to have all these things to do so we could avoid further conversation. We couldn't go to the usual Tube platform, of course, so we walked a block to a public shelter. I told myself that statistically it was unlikely a bomb would hit me again. We sat on a wooden bench and Dad stared at the people. I had to remind myself that this was all new to him – making me feel as though I were the adult, not him. The raid didn't last as long as usual and the action seemed to be further to the west. We were home again before eleven.

'How many times have you had to do this?' he asked, unlocking the door to our flat.

I tried to count but couldn't remember.

'You seem so unruffled by the bombs.' There was pride on his face but I still couldn't bear to let myself feel any warmth towards him. 'Despite what happened to you in that Tube station.'

'You just get used to it.' Even to myself, I sounded cool.

In the morning I went out first thing to buy milk. When I came back Dad was already up, reading a book by the window. His face brightened when he saw me.

'Breakfast with my daughter. I've dreamed of this.'

I grunted.

'Shall I lay the table, darling?'

'I can manage, thanks.'

But he stood up and came over to me, placing his hands on my shoulders. 'I can't tell you everything, Rachel. You'll have to trust me until I can.' He spoke quite crisply. I blinked. 'So let's try and get on with one another, shall we? Until we can talk openly.'

'When will that be?' I knew I must sound sulky, grudging.

'Not long now.'

We ate in silence, but the silence didn't feel so uncomfortable. Perhaps the charges against Dad had been false ones and Inspector Blake was helping to clear his name so we could tell the world he was no traitor.

Dad was going to see Mum again and I had to visit Mrs H, who needed fresh clothes taking to her. I left my beret at home and pulled up my raincoat collar, letting my hair flop over my face as I walked to the bus stop. Just in case O'Leary was looking out for me.

The bus route took me south over Westminister Bridge. I sat with my head in an algebra book, hoping this too would make it harder for O'Leary and his repulsive white dog to spot me.

To my delight I found Mrs H already dressed and preparing for discharge, with just one bandage above her wrist.

'Rachel! They decided I was taking up a bed that would be better used by someone else and should go home to rest. I'm so pleased to see you.' She looked at my temple.

'It's nothing,' I told her.

She grabbed my hand as though to reassure herself I was really there.

'I'm sorry I didn't get to see you yesterday.' I explained about Dad's release. Her eyes shone.

'How wonderful, Rachel.'

'I still don't understand any of it.'

'Perhaps it wasn't as bad as you fear. Anyone can make a mistake about a political party. Thousands in Germany have done the same.'

'I suppose so.'

I couldn't help feeling more cheerful just by being with her again. Then I remembered I still had something to tell her, something sad. About Perseus. I tried to do it gently, saying I had bad news. She turned white.

'It's Ernst, isn't it? He's got pneumonia in that camp?'

'No, no –'

'Your mother? That fever of hers. Dear God, she's got an infection. I told that sister –'

'It's not a human.' Then she knew. The tight grip on my wrist relaxed.

'Perseus?'

'I'm so sorry.'

She closed her eyes briefly.

'I've been telling myself he's an old bird, that he wouldn't last much longer, especially now we can't buy the right food for him.'

Why tell her it had been deliberate? Why give her the added pain? She might think the budgie had died from shock. That happened to pets in air raids.

I'd put the body into a shoebox lined with a handkerchief, ready for burial. I'd forced myself to arrange the bird so his poor neck didn't look so obviously broken. Let Mrs H think it was a natural death.

She pulled a pristine white handkerchief out of her sleeve. 'He had a good life. Who knows what would have become of him if we'd left him in Germany?'

Could it have been worse than having his neck broken by some bigoted, ignorant Londoner? I told her about the missing tea-spoons too. She sighed and shrugged. 'I suppose I should be glad they didn't take the really valuable things.' She'd be thinking of that Cubist painting.

We made our way out of the bustling hospital to catch the bus back. For the length of the journey I continued to keep an eye out for the Irishman and his dog, scanning passengers as they boarded the bus. But would he dare approach me in daylight, in public? I remembered that gun and shivered.

'Do you have a fever too?' Mrs H was watching me.

'I'm fine.' In fact, for all the fear I felt about what O'Leary might do next, for all the concern about my mother and my complete incomprehension of my father's actions, I'd never felt physically better. I'd hardly scratched my skin at all this morning.

We got off the bus in Tottenham Court Road and walked the short distance to Fulton Street.

My stray was waiting at the steps to the house. I found half a piece of toast I'd saved from breakfast and stuffed into my raincoat pocket and gave it to him. He deserved it, and more. Even a fillet steak wouldn't have been enough reward for the dog. Mrs H shook her head but didn't tell me off.

I took her up to her flat. She glanced at the shoebox on the table and at the empty birdcage, which I'd cleaned out. But she said nothing. I prayed that if and when she examined the small corpse she wouldn't notice the floppy head.

'Shall I put on the kettle?'

'That would be most kind. And now I must write to Ernst.' She looked older this afternoon. I noticed the little web of lines around her eyes.

'Would you like me to do any shopping for you?'

'You're a kind girl, Rachel, a good girl. But I think a little fresh air after lunch might do me good.'

Dad was writing letters in our living room. Nothing needed doing in the flat and I felt no urge to do equations so I decided to try and find Paul Gabriel. My need to see him had grown more compelling than my fear of O'Leary. I had to know what hold this man had over him. Paul was no saint, but O'Leary was evil. They didn't belong together.

I set off towards the Tube station, glancing over my shoulder from time to time in case I was being followed. If Paul didn't show up there I'd move on to Windmill Street. Chances were he'd pass one of our meeting places at some point today.

And there he was, striding out as though he owned the city. He saw me.

'Hello.'

'Hello.' I felt suddenly shy. I'd promised to stay indoors, out of danger. But I hadn't. 'I needed some exercise,' I said in self-justification.

'You know it's dangerous.'

'Where are you going?' I asked.

'Business.'

'May I come with you?'

He frowned.

'At least you'd know I was safe.'

He raised an eyebrow. 'That's one way of putting it. Look, Rachel, you've seen what O'Leary's like now, don't you think you'd be better off –'

'Please don't treat me like a child.'

'All right.'

His business took us west to a photographer's shop in Marylebone. Was he going to have a portrait taken or something? Paul reached inside his black coat and placed two cans of film on the counter. The shopkeeper looked down his nose.

'Wrong stock. I sell cameras, son. Why don't you try the film boys down Wardour Street?' He picked up one of the cans and examined it.

'Where did you get those from, anyway?' I knew he'd have stolen them.

Paul shrugged and reached for the cans.

'Like you say, I should try Wardour Street.'

'Hang on.' The shopkeeper kept his hand on the can he'd picked up. 'Never said I weren't interested. Two pounds.'

'Four.'

'Three.'

'Done.'

'Where are we going now?' I asked when we were back on the street.

'You ask a lot of questions.' He touched his pocket. 'There's something I need to . . . dispose of.'

'What?'

He waited whole seconds before he pulled something out of his trouser pocket.

'If you really want to know, this is what I do. This is what I took.' On his palm a ring glinted gold, blue and white: a diamond-and-sapphire ring.

'Where did you get it?' But I'd already guessed. He'd taken it from some dead girl's finger. Probably one of the dancers at the night-club that had been bombed. This ring must still have been warm when he'd pulled it off. I wanted to retch. He must have seen the look on my face because he clenched his fingers round the ring to hide it.

'Told you you wouldn't like it.'

'Do you really need cash so badly?' I asked it gently. He'd told me what I needed to know, what was between him and O'Leary.

I expected he'd sneer at me but he replaced the ring in his pocket and looked me in the eye.

'I owe O'Leary twenty pounds. That's why he's after me.'

'Twenty pounds!'

'He lent me money when my sister went to Australia. She needed clothes so she didn't go off looking like a beggar. Mum and Gran would have hated that. And we owed the landlord and the local shopkeeper. There were other debts too.' He looked away. 'O'Leary wants me to take that painting to a dealer for him. Well, a pawnbroker, more like.'

I didn't know what a pawnbroker was. He must have seen the ignorance in my face.

'People who need readies take things to the pawnbroker and he lends them money against the value of the goods. If they can't repay the debt he sells their stuff.' He peered at me. 'You hadn't heard of them?'

I shook my head. I'd learned about girls going behind bombed buildings with men. And about looters searching houses. And people selling black-market goods in back-street pubs. But not about pawnbrokers, until now.

'What sort of things do they sell?'

'All sorts. Clocks, watches, jewellery, silver. Sometimes even their false teeth.'

A whole world unknown to me until now. Would I have learned about people selling their false teeth if I'd gone to that boarding school? I doubted it.

'And you don't want to take the painting to the pawnbroker because there's something fishy about it?'

He nodded, rubbing the toe of his brown suede shoe against the pavement.

'I don't like it and I don't want anything to do with that house. That's why I need to sell the ring. The cans of film didn't fetch much.' He'd made a mark on the dusty pavement like a cross. 'You don't need to be involved. Go home.'

'I want to save you,' I blurted out.

'Save me!' He gave a single savage burst of laughter. 'Who d'you think you are? The bleeding Sally Army? The Virgin Mary?'

'You don't need to live like this. You're clever. You could take classes.'

'I want to join up.' He said the words in such a low tone it took me a second to work out what they were.

'The army?'

'Why not?' He glared, as though daring me to mock. 'Or perhaps the navy. Not that either of them would give me more than skivvy work. I haven't got those bits of paper that show you can think.'

'And you're too young.'

'Not for much longer. And this war's going to go on for a while yet.'

'Another good reason to stop stealing things. They won't let you join up if you've got a criminal record. They'll make you mop barrack floors or peel potatoes.' I knew I was being cruel but I wanted him to see that he had to stop.

He leaned back against the boarding, looking smaller and younger. 'If O'Leary would just leave me alone I'd be fine. I could find casual work till I'm old enough to join up. The police haven't got anything on me at the moment. Just one caution and that was years ago.'

'How'd you get involved with that dreadful man in the first place?'

He glanced sideways at me. 'I can't even remember how he came to know us. I was doing odd jobs for a rag-and-bone man after school, going through piles of scrap metal in case there was anything special that could be sold on. O'Leary used to come to the yard. We got talking.'

I frowned, trying to picture the immaculately suited figure in the grubby surroundings of a scrap-metal business.

'He wasn't so smart in those days,' Paul added. 'He'd ask me to sort through the piles and he'd pick out bits and pieces. While he was doing it he'd chat to me, ask me about my family. Give me oranges and stuff sometimes. He said I reminded him of himself at that age. My dad was gone and I . . .'

'Missed having a man around?' I certainly knew the feeling. Paul nodded.

'One thing led to another. I started doing jobs for O'Leary after school, delivering things for him. 'I didn't know that most of what I was taking was stolen goods. By the time I was thirteen I'd probably broken the law a dozen times without realising. Gran would have belted me, if she'd known. And now.' He shrugged. 'If he squeals to the coppers, I'm done for.'

'I can give you seventeen pounds to pay him off,' I said. 'Then, with the three you got for the film, you'd have enough. And you could hand in the ring to the police, say you found it.'

Doubt flickered over his face.

'I could take it to the station. They wouldn't think I'd stolen it.'

His lips twitched. 'You're right there, Miss Pearse.'

I ignored the amusement in his voice. 'And you could tell O'Leary to leave you alone.'

'But have you really got seventeen quid?'

'In my post office account.' People had given me money for birthdays and Christmas and I hadn't always needed to spend it. Over the years it had built up. Mum called it my nest egg.

'Don't you need a signature?'

'Dad would sign it if I said I needed the cash for clothes or something.'

'Seventeen pounds on clothes! You're joking.'

I thought about it. 'I'll ask him to sign the form before I fill in the amount.'

He nodded, then looked confused. 'Just a moment, you said your dad'll sign it? Did they let him out? You didn't tell me about this.'

I explained.

'You must be pleased.' He studied my face.

'He doesn't seem very sorry,' I said.

'Perhaps it wasn't as bad as you thought.' The near-repeat of Mrs H's words made me blink. 'What about your mum? How's she doing now?'

'Her temperature's down. She's happy that Dad is back.' I said it all mechanically. Of course it was good that Mum was so happy. Dad's being home might help her recover. But I didn't want to think about my father now.

'Getting back to the money,' Paul said, 'it would take me months and months to pay you back. Years, perhaps.'

'That wouldn't matter. I trust you.'

The green eyes widened. 'Do you?'

I shrugged. 'I think you'd pay me back.'

'I would.'

I took his arm. 'C'mon, give me the ring so I can hand it in.'

'Not to Inspector Blake, though?'

'Do you think I'm an idiot? He won't be on the desk, will he? It'll be some lowly sergeant.'

He glanced at his watch. 'It's already two o'clock. O'Leary will be out looking for me. I'll slip the money under the door of his lodgings while he's out and then hole up in that big public shelter down Tilbury way till he leaves town. He won't want to hang around now Inspector Blake is moving in on him.'

I held out my hand for the ring and when he handed it to me I put it on my finger, covering my hands with my gloves. 'I'll go to the post office on the way to see Mum.'

We walked briskly east towards Fulton Street.

'There's the post office.' I pointed at it. 'Meet you there at quarter to three.' He grabbed me before I could stride off. 'What's happening?' His answer was to glance over his shoulder and pull me into a narrow strip running between a bombed shop and its neighbour. His mouth was on mine again before I could say a word.

This time his exploring tongue met mine quickly. His hand ran inside my coat, found the buttons on my shirt, undid one or two and explored further. There wasn't much to explore, to be honest, but he didn't seem to mind, finishing his journey round my chest area with a little sigh and a kiss to my brow. All very quick, but sweet. And right. Mum and Dad and Inspector Blake probably wouldn't have agreed, but I certainly hadn't been thinking about them during the last few minutes.

'You can trust me, Rachel,' he said. 'God knows, most people wouldn't. Taking that girl's ring, that was bad. I know it was bad. Even at the time I knew. I'm finished with this kind of life.'

22

I ran back along the street, feeling my face flushing for reasons that had nothing to do with eczema.

I found Dad in the living room, finishing his correspondence. He pushed the letters under the writing pad as I came in.

'There you are.' He nodded at my gloved hands. 'Does the cold hurt your poor hands?'

'A little.' I smiled at him. 'Dad, I need money to buy some stuff. What with Mum in hospital.' I tailed off. His cheeks turned pink. I could only imagine what he was thinking I might need. He wouldn't want to enquire further.

'You don't need to use your own money for essentials.' He reached for the wallet on the desk beside the writing pad. 'How much do you need?' I couldn't let my father bail out Paul Gabriel.

'Quite a bit. I need clothes for, erm, parties.' He looked pleased at the idea of someone inviting me to a party. If he'd been back in London for longer he'd have known that the number of parties someone my age was likely to attend was very small as so many people had been evacuated. 'I think I should use my savings. You always said they were for rainy days.'

'But have you got enough coupons?'

If this interrogation went on much longer I'd miss the post office. 'Yes.'

'How much do you want to take out?'

'Five pounds,' I lied. Before the war I'd have died rather than tell lies to my father. But if he was going to be less than honest with himself and us about his political past it absolved me from the need to be truthful. I went into my bedroom and found the little book and slip you needed a parent to sign and gave both to him. He took his fountain pen and signed.

'You haven't filled in the amount.'

'I forgot. I'll do it now.' I stood with my back to him and filled in the real amount. Then I found an old envelope in a kitchen drawer and wrote 'FOR THE ATTENTION OF INSPECTOR BLAKE' on it in capitals, crudely formed and backward slanting. 'I'll be back in half an hour, in plenty of time for visiting Mum.'

He gave me his old smile.

I thought of Mrs H's Cubist painting, with its many-sided woman. My father had also revealed himself as multi-faceted: no longer the purely and simply wonderful father of my childhood. Perhaps this was what being adult meant, accepting that nothing and nobody was ever just one thing. We all had different sides, choosing to show whichever one suited the circumstances.

I couldn't see a letter box on the police station door so I had to walk inside, praying the inspector wouldn't be around. The desk sergeant had his back to me, talking to a constable about the difficulties of obtaining decent lamb chops these days. I slipped the envelope under the grille and crept out without him turning round.

Paul hadn't reached the post office when I went inside with my account book and slip. The lady behind the counter frowned at me.

'This seems rather a lot of money, young lady. People are supposed to be putting surplus funds into war bonds, not taking out cash.' She might have been Hitler himself, telling people what they could do with their own money.

'I need new clothes,' I told her. 'I keep growing. And I lost all my school things when our school was bombed. I've got the coupons.' That shut up the old bag while she counted out the notes for me.

Paul was waiting outside. I pulled him away from the post office window in case she was still watching.

'Here.'

He swallowed as he took the notes. 'Rachel – '

'Got to go. I'll miss visiting time.' I didn't want him to tell me he was grateful or sorry or whatever. 'Let's try and meet tomorrow.'

'What about outside the Tube at quarter to two?'

'Yes,' I called as I ran off.

23

'Did you find O'Leary?' I asked as soon as we met the next afternoon.

Paul dug his hands into his coat pockets and shook his head. 'I went to his lodgings and he was out. The landlady was hanging round and I didn't like to leave the money. She's a bit rough. Didn't want her to nick it.'

'So what will you do?'

'Wait until night. O'Leary usually goes back to the lodgings for supper. I'll stick it under his door when I'm certain he's there.'

'So what now?' I felt uneasy. I'd hoped this business would have been resolved by this afternoon.

'Quick stroll?'

I looked at my watch. 'I've got a bit of time before I need to be at the hospital to visit Mum.'

We ambled through streets of crumpled buildings and boarded windows. London looked worse every day. Until now I hadn't really noticed just how much it was crumbling away. It was no longer poetically sad, just depressing.

'Penny for them?' Paul asked.

I told him about the bombed buildings, how they'd reminded me of poems I'd once read, back in the times when I'd just been a silly kid who knew nothing. I expected him to laugh when I described how I felt about the ruins, but he didn't.

'I feel like that about trees in autumn.' He nodded at a lone beech on a street corner, its leaves the colour of a new penny. 'But at least you know they'll be back in leaf next spring.'

I liked the way he talked about next spring, as though we'd both be around to see it and as though the tree would, too. Sometimes it seemed as if death and sadness would take over the whole world.

We continued in companionable silence, turning back into Tottenham Court Road and walking on past a shop selling lino for floors. Not that they were selling much lino these days.

'I could murder for a cup of tea and a bun,' I said. 'Dad was out and I didn't have any lunch. My treat.'

'Was that what you had before the war – tea and buns?'

'Why do you ask?'

He shrugged. 'No reason. Just interested in how you lived then.'

I tried to remember. 'I liked Battenberg cake. You know, the pink-and-yellow one.'

'Battenberg,' he repeated to himself. 'Sounds German. Where the hell can you get Battenberg cake these days?'

'Probably nowhere.'

'There's a baker's a few blocks up. Let's try.'

'It doesn't matter,' I said. 'I'm happy with a bun.'

He shook his head. 'Let's try and make it special.'

We peered at the shop windows and at the shoppers bustling past, housewives anxious and tired-looking, Canadian soldiers handsome in their uniform. At Johnson's baker's shop Paul halted. 'This used to be good, I've heard.'

We went inside and he winked at the shop-keeper. 'Battenberg cake.'

'You'll be lucky. Try Fortnum's.'

I pulled out a half-crown. 'Not even just two thin slices?'

The baker raised his eyebrows. 'I'll have a look.' Nobody was talking ration books.

He reappeared from the back of the shop with two thin squares of the chequered cake. 'Soft as a duchess's behind.' He grinned at me.

'That all you got?' Paul asked. 'Don't seem much for the money.'

'The rest's promised for a tea party in Swiss Cottage. I don't have any cake boxes for that slice. You'll have to manage without. At a time – '

'Like this,' I finished for him.

'What about a small tin?' Paul asked.

'You don't ask for much, do you?' He rummaged around under the counter and pulled out a rectangular tin. 'This do?'

'It's an old tobacco tin,' I said. 'It'll make the cake smell of cigarettes.'

'It's fine. Smell it.'

I raised it to my nostrils and nodded.

'You kids,' said the baker. 'You don't know you're born. You don't know there's a war on.'

Paul picked up the tin. 'I'll carry this for you.' He placed it in his inside pocket. 'Let's find a bench somewhere.' The feeble sun was trying to break through the clouds and the afternoon had almost turned into a jaunt.

We turned a corner. There was O'Leary. With the dog. He nodded towards a side street. I looked around. The crowds had thinned out. Nobody was there to witness what might happen. O'Leary could pull out a gun and nobody would see. We followed him to a heap of rubble behind a cinema. O'Leary held the dog's lead tight so the collar strained against the animal's thick neck. The pale hair on its hackles rose.

'I've been looking everywhere for you, Paulie.'

'I'll pay you your money.' Paul took out the notes, counting them in front of the Ulsterman and stuffing them into his gnarled hand. 'There.'

'You've been busy. I thought the bombed nightclub would be too good an opportunity for you to pass.' O'Leary examined the money. 'All those fat wallets, all those bracelets and rings.'

'You've got your cash, now we're off.' Paul's face wore an expression of relief and lightness. He was finally free of O'Leary and it was only now that I really saw how much this meant to him.

The older man moved more quickly than I'd have thought possible and grabbed Paul's shoulder. 'Listen to me, Paulie, there's no time for mucking around. We're not finished yet.' The dog growled, showing its yellow teeth.

'We're finished all right.'

'Have you forgotten all I did for you in the past?'

'I've just paid you back every penny.'

'You think it's enough just to stuff a handful of cash into my palm? To treat me like someone you haven't known for years? Someone who cared for you, who helped you?'

'You only used me to help yourself.'

'Now you're just being ungrateful.'

Paul shrugged. O'Leary was watching him closely. His tone altered, became more threatening.

'And there's interest, Paulie, interest.'

'What are you talking about, interest? You never mentioned interest before.'

'One last little job, that's all I ask.' O'Leary softened his voice. 'Something else I can flog for a quick profit. That should cover the outstanding amount.'

'We're off.' Paul's firm tones made the dog growl again. 'C'mon, Rachel.'

O'Leary seemed to notice me for the first time. 'How are you this afternoon, missy?' He put out a yellow-nailed hand and stroked my hair. I took a step back to evade the touch. 'Nice-looking girl. Lives on Fulton Street, doesn't she? In the house where they kept that bloody Kraut budgie.'

Paul stepped towards us. 'Keep away from her.'

I was feeling nauseous. O'Leary had been to our house, to Mrs H's flat. Had it been him who'd killed Perseus? The bird's death had had nothing to do with the German words he'd cheeped. It had been a warning. He'd strangled the budgie and pocketed Mrs H's teaspoons at the same time because he was a dirty thief who couldn't resist a quick and easy robbery. Presumably the heavier pieces of silver in the flat had proved too hard for him to secrete on himself. And he obviously wasn't very knowledgeable about modern art or he'd have taken Mrs H's Cubist painting. Maybe he was above carrying heavy loads of stolen property and had thought of sending Paul around to collect the other objects for him.

I imagined O'Leary creeping upstairs and into our own flat and told myself I'd lock both front doors with my own hand tonight when the alert sounded and not trust to Dad or Mrs H.

'Don't let me down,' he was telling Paul. 'Bring something nice to the usual place before the raids start.'

'Scared of the Heinkels, are you?'

'I've got a train to catch.' O'Leary glared at Paul and then at me. 'I've kept Flynn under control but he's still very restless. Lack of exercise. There was an incident in Belfast. A child's cheek was bitten. Not really the dog's fault but the little boy's mother didn't see it like that.' His eyes locked on mine. 'And dogs have good memories, you know. If someone stabs them with a carving knife, they'll remember.'

'If you touch her – '

O'Leary laughed. 'Come over all heroic, have we, Paulie?'

'It's the last time.'

'That's what you said at White City.'

'The night you bladed a man through his liver because he didn't do what you wanted?'

'Dog racing's a rough sport.' O'Leary rubbed his hands. 'So's war. Too rough for you, it seems.'

'I'm joining up as soon as I'm old enough.'

'There's a patriot in there after all, is there?' O'Leary bared grey teeth. 'Find me something nice from one of those abandoned houses, Paulie. Perhaps a nice painting, like the one your lady friend told you about.'

Paul's lady friend?

'If you know the painting's there why don't you just take it yourself?' Paul asked.

O'Leary's answer was just another of his chilling smiles.

'Don't want to run the risk of being caught with it yourself, do you?'

'It's heavier than it looks. And I'm not as fit as I used to be.' O'Leary clicked his tongue at the dog. 'Remember who owes whom what, Paulie. Else Flynn and I may need to pay Rachel here a few visits to remind her about the dangers of keeping scum like you company.'

Man and dog were gone. We stood in silence, digesting what O'Leary had said.

The afternoon light was already waning and I hadn't visited Mum yet. Paul Gabriel needed to find something fast. The painting in Lord Street would do. I knew he was thinking about the same thing. It seemed fate had intended the painted girl for him. But something else was pre-occupying me.

'Who's this lady friend?'

Paul seemed to spot something in the gutter that needed his attention. 'Nobody. Just a friend.'

'It didn't sound like that.'

His cheeks turned slightly pink and he stuck his hands in his pockets, staring in the direction O'Leary had gone.

'Her name's Irena. She's a refugee. She's got rooms in the same place I live.'

I'd expected – hoped – he'd tell me it was all just a lie made up by O'Leary. 'I see.' I could make visiting time if I left now. 'Well, good luck with everything.'

'Rachel –' He grabbed at my arm but I jumped clear.

'It doesn't matter to me who you see.' I sounded airy, unbothered. 'And please don't feel you have to protect me. I live above a police inspector, after all.'

But I remembered the budgie.

'O'Leary got it wrong, there's nothing between Irena and me.'

'But she told you about the painting and that's what made you take it? I always wondered exactly how you came to know about it.'

'I don't have feelings for Irena. It's not like that.'

I shrugged. 'None of my business, anyway.' I walked away, being sure to keep my shoulders back and not to hurry.

24

'They want me to go to a convalescence home on the south coast.' Mum looked better this afternoon. Not too pale. Or too flushed. She sat up straighter in bed rather than slumping – as though healthy blood coursed through her veins, healing her battered body.

'Sounds like a good idea,' Dad said. 'We could afford to send you somewhere nice.'

I looked at him. I'd been assuming that our days of having money were over. He seemed to read my mind.

'I'll be earning decent money again, Rachel. Not like I was before . . . what happened, but enough to keep us more comfortably. No more living in scruffy flats for us.'

I felt a pang at the prospect of leaving Fulton Street with its untidy window boxes and errant dustbins. And Paul Gabriel. I brushed away thoughts of him. It was over between us.

'It would mean we'd have to review the school options again.' Mum spoke quietly. 'Your father will be working in Berkshire, Rachel. I'll be in the south. You obviously can't stay in London alone.'

'Mrs Hoffman – '

'Can't really be expected to take any more responsibility for you, darling,' Mum said. 'It's not fair to ask her.'

'And there's your education,' Dad went on. 'You're doing wonderfully keeping your maths going, but there's history, French, science, music.'

I said nothing. That wretched boarding school in freezing, remote Lincolnshire. If they were going to send me there I'd be better off blasted to pieces in an air raid.

'What about finding a school near the lab which takes day and boarding pupils?' Dad said. 'Then, when your mother's better, you can both live with me and you won't have to board.'

A reprieve. The old me wanted to kick up a fuss, refuse to consider boarding, even temporarily. But I could see their point.

'As long as the boarding bit isn't permanent.'

'It won't be.' Mum patted my hand. 'You're a funny girl. Some people your age would be desperate for boarding school. Midnight feasts and games – ' She broke off, laughing at my disgusted face. It was good to hear her laugh.

'You've grown up a lot, Rachel.' Dad was looking at me. 'Not the little girl you were before I . . . left.'

'Yeah, well,' I growled. 'There's been a lot going on.'

The bell rang to mark the end of visiting time. I rose, anxious to leave before the obnoxious sister had the pleasure of kicking me out, which would upset Mum. Dad wanted to buy tobacco on the way home so I said I'd meet him back at the flat.

The siren sounded when I was about a block away from home. I decided to dash in quickly and fetch my bedding, and my algebra so I'd have something to keep me occupied in the shelter. I was glad Dad wouldn't come down with me. He'd volunteered for fire-watching duty and would be busy tonight. No looking for Paul Gabriel tonight. He could get his precious girlfriend to help if he needed assistance.

A few planes buzzed overhead. Behind me I heard a rustling sound which I knew was that of falling incendiaries. I reached our front door, stopped and sniffed the air. Something was burning. I looked around, couldn't see it. Then I heard a crackle above me and located the source. An incendiary must have landed on the fire escape and the sparks had set alight the basket of laundry I'd left outside. 'Damn!'

We kept buckets of sand on each landing inside the building. I ran upstairs to our floor, grabbing the fire bucket as I went. I ran through to the kitchen and opened the door. The washing was now well alight. The still-healing skin on my hands seemed to burn as I approached. I threw sand over the burning clothes but it was too late: already flames were licking our kitchen door. I needed water. I ran back through the back door, making for the sink.

Arms grabbed me in the kitchen.

'Well done. We'll take over from here.' My father. 'The engine's on the way now.'

I could barely hear him now. Fleets of bombers rumbled in the sky. Explosives had replaced the incendiaries, banging and thumping to the south over New Oxford Street. It was so noisy I only heard the fire engine's bell when it was directly outside the house. I went to the living-room window to watch. A young woman in dungarees jumped out and unwound a hose. I heard her shout a question about water hydrants. Another vehicle had pulled up beside it: a big black car. Must be someone important.

Inspector Blake got out.

'Rachel! Off to the shelter.' Dad took me by the arm. 'I can't believe you're still hanging around here.'

'I just wanted to get my books.'

'Hurry.' He paused at the door. 'Oh, and well done, darling. You probably helped save this whole building. I'm proud of you.'

I was pleased, despite my reservations about my father. I walked downstairs with my blanket and satchel, pleasure giving me a warm tingle inside.

'Evening, Rachel.' Inspector Blake nodded at me. 'Off to the shelter. Good.'

He looked very pleased with himself. I muttered something and was about to walk off when a constable approached. I couldn't make out what he said but suddenly car doors were slamming and I could hear the roar of the engine over the din of planes and anti-aircraft. As they passed me Inspector Blake wound down his window. 'Make sure you go straight to the shelter,' he called.

Why was he so keen to get me off the streets? Something was going on. There could be only one reason for the big car driving around in the middle of a raid.

Inspector Blake was about to make an arrest.

25

I had to find Paul. At the junction with Tottenham Court Road I came to a halt, planes screeching above me, flares flashing over the sky. What should I do?

I'd acted like a jealous kid, just because O'Leary, of all people, had mentioned this Irena person. Suppose Paul had been telling the truth about her? Suppose they *were* just friends?

Whatever the situation, I had to warn Paul. He was too close to making a break with O'Leary. It would be too cruel for him to be brought down just because he was in the wrong place tonight. If he could get away and hide out in a big public shelter the police might forget about him. He could make his way on to somewhere remote. Or perhaps a large northern city with plenty of factory jobs on offer would be better. Whatever my doubts about him I couldn't just leave him in trouble.

I felt perspiration beading my brow. How on earth could I find him? The first place I thought of was the Blue Lion in Windmill Street. As pedestrians ran for the shelter I turned in the opposite direction, towards the pub.

The landlord gave his full attention to the glass he was polishing as, in answer to my question, he told me he had no idea where Paul Gabriel would be tonight. 'Which is exactly the answer I gave the cops when they asked me, too,' he added, rubbing the greasy cloth round the glass's rim.

'Where does he live?' I pleaded.

'I run a bleeding pub not a directory service.'

'Please?'

Some men playing darts nudged one another and came closer. I flushed.

'Try York Street, love,' one of them called. 'Above a coffee shop, I think he said.'

'You find him, love, and take his mind off the bombs,' said his friend, smirking at me.

'Thank you.' I hurried out of the pub, the taunts of the darts players following me, their mocking eyes burning my back. I'd come out without gloves or hat and the temperature had dropped. No time to return to the flat for warmer clothes. At least my hands didn't throb in the cold the way they once had.

The clouds had cleared. Another perfect night for the bombers, still swarming in the sky. I wrapped my coat around me and broke into a run, causing an elderly man to sidestep into a shop doorway and raise his hat at me.

Rushing through the gloom I might get to Gabriel's flat in minutes but I'd be lucky if I got there without breaking a bone. Once or twice I nearly ran off the edge of the kerb or tripped on an uneven and invisible paving stone. This was a fool's errand. I couldn't hope to find Paul before Inspector Blake did.

I stopped to take my bearings by the side of a bombed-out church. It was – or had been – a Catholic church. A plaster Virgin stared down from the one remaining wall, a small vase of chrysanthemums beneath it. I shivered and looked away from her.

A large car pulled out of a side street and threw its hooded lights on to a poster advertising St Bruno Tobacco. The thin beams moved on to a poster on a glass window informing shoppers the store no longer sold coffee beans or ground coffee. This must be Paul's place. Paint peeled on the red door. I pushed the single bell. It took so long for someone to come I was about to walk off when I heard footsteps coming downstairs and the door opened.

An elegant girl three or four years older than I was stood in front of me. I hadn't expected someone like this – someone so poised, examining me with the edges of her mouth turned up. I'm not sure what exactly I had expected, but not this. She was slightly shorter than me, with hair falling in neat, glossy waves to her shoulders. 'I was looking for Paul Gabriel.' My words sounded uncertain.

'He's not here.' She had a slight accent: central European, perhaps.

'I . . . It's important that I find him.' The girl's brown eyebrows formed two neat question marks. A bomb screamed as it fell through the air close by. She pulled her cardigan more tightly around her.

'Nearest shelter's back that way.' She pointed past the church and started to close the door.

'Please.' I put a hand out to stop her. 'He's in trouble.'

She considered the words. 'Well, you'd better come in.' I followed her up a steep, narrow staircase. The carpet had come away from the treads. A group of framed photographs of European beauty spots hung crookedly on the wall.

The young woman motioned me into the living room. A half-packed suitcase lay on a chair.

'Sit down.' Although the words were curt there was something gracious in the way she waited for me to sit before sitting herself that made me look again at her. As though reading my mind the woman smiled. *I'm not what you think,* that smile said. I turned my hands over in my lap so that she couldn't see the backs of them.

'Paul said he was going up to Marylebone this afternoon. I don't know where he was going afterwards.' Her words were almost expression-less but something in her eyes made me study her more closely. I could discover nothing in that composed face. 'Perhaps Lord Street?' She glanced at me, eyes slightly narrowed.

I flushed at the mention of that place. 'My name's Rachel Pearse.' I wanted to see if there were any flicker of recognition. Her face relaxed and she almost seemed to laugh momentarily.

'I met your father, Professor Pearse, today. You have the same eyes as him.'

I stared at her as though she was mad.

26

'You can't have met him,' I said.

'Oh, but I have.' She seemed amused by my astonishment. 'Your father is – ' An explosion thundered across the street. I found myself clutching the arms of the chair. Irena rose. 'This isn't safe. We go to the shelter now, yes?'

I could barely hear her through the pounding and thumping of explosives – as though a giant had upturned a bag of enormous wooden balls – and followed her downstairs, clutching the banister as the house trembled. At the front door she paused, a hand held out to stop me from opening it.

'No time for the shelter. We'll go into the cellar.' She pointed at a door at the back of the entrance hall. 'Hurry.' She unbolted the door and opened it, revealing dark, damp steps.

'No.' I felt my stomach turn over. 'I can't go down there.' I backed away from the doorway.

'You must!' The ceiling shook.

'No!' I was backing away. Anything rather than that shadowy subterranean hidey-hole where we might be buried alive. Nobody knew where I was. They mightn't ever find my body. She shook her head and started to walk down the dark steps. I grabbed her sleeve. 'Tell me why you know my father?' My voice was hoarse from shouting against the roar of the raid.

'Do you know Paul Gabriel steals rings off dead girls' fingers?' she said, as though in answer.

'Yes.'

Irena raised an inquisitive eyebrow. 'And it doesn't worry you?' She sounded almost amused.

'Tell me about my father!'

A low crumping moan turned into a thunderous roar and crack. Irena grabbed my arm and forced me down the cellar steps. Bricks, timbers and plaster crashed down in a single sshhhooopp to the spot where I'd been standing just a second earlier. It looked as though most of the ceiling had fallen in. I found myself clutching Irena. She was muttering words I couldn't understand: prayers in German or Czech or whatever language it was. We waited. Dust and fragments of plaster dropped ground-wards. 'Are you hurt?' she asked me.

'No.'

'We were lucky.' She put a hand to her sleek hair and brushed off dust.

The planes must have moved a mile or two away. I could still hear the droning of their engines but the explosions were more distant now.

Irena and I walked back up the steps into the entrance hall. She gazed up at the hole above us. 'This is dangerous, more could fall down on us any second. This is an old house and nobody has taken care of it. We go now.' She wrapped her cardigan round her slender shoulders. 'I already have my ID and ration card.' She patted her skirt pocket. 'I am never without them.'

'You'll freeze without a coat.'

She shrugged. 'Come, we find the shelter.'

I followed her out on to the street. 'Tell me about my father?'

'If you don't know, you weren't meant to know.'

'Is it something to do with the Isle of Man?' We could hear one another without raising our voices now.

She glanced sideways at me.

'You don't know everything about your father's imprisonment. In fact, Rachel, you probably know very little.' She didn't say it in a patronising way but her words still made me bristle. 'He did it for *them*,' she went on.

'Who?'

'The government. The state. England, whatever you call it.' She sounded surprised at my slowness. 'To see what was being said, and to whom. To try and find out if there are enemies within this country.'

My father – some kind of agent? I couldn't take it in.

'So how is it that you know him?'

She looked away from me.

'Are you one of them too? An undercover agent or spy?'

She gave me a thin smile. 'I come from the German part of Czechoslovakia. Many Germans there support Hitler, but not me. My father was a dissenting church minister, a man of God who hated the Nazis. He's in a camp now.'

I started to say that I was sorry. She shook her hand, dismissing my condolences.

'It's why I came here a few years ago. Your intelligence service used me to find out what was happening in the German community over here.'

I thought again of Inspector Blake in his big black car, flushing out O'Leary. And Paul. This whole business was so hard to comprehend, so unbelievable, like something from a thriller. But then I remembered that snippet of conversation between Dad and Inspector Blake. Dad had told the inspector how much he was looking forward to going back to his work. His work: his real job, not the temporary work that had taken him away from us for all these months. I glanced at Irena. She seemed sane enough not to have made up this whole thing.

She turned to me and a flare showed me the directness of her hazel stare. 'Your father is a good man. He gave up a lot to do this work.'

'So did we.' I thought of our home packed up, our dog sent away, the boarding-school plan, our family fractured. She nodded.

'It is hard for the families.'

'I thought . . . Well, I was starting to have doubts about my father. They said he was a traitor.' Even as I said the words I realised how ridiculous the whole thing had been. Dad, a man who'd found jobs in his laboratory for scientists fleeing the Continent, a supporter of Hitler, Franco and Mussolini! Dad, who was so uninterested in politics he could hardly bring himself to vote in elections. How could I have imagined him as a Blackshirt?

She shook her head, as though marvelling at my naivety, too. 'The intelligence people asked me to provide them with names of possible spies. I think that's what your father was doing in the internment camp: looking for names of people they hadn't arrested yet.'

'Like O'Leary?'

She halted. 'Did Paul tell you about him?' Something had changed in her at the mention of that name.

'I've met him myself.' I shivered, remembering the gun. And that dog. She took my arm.

'Listen, Rachel, O'Leary is a very, very dangerous man. I don't know if he's really a spy or just a gangster.' She sounded different now, the cool poise gone. 'He's killed people. Stay away from him. And from Paul. Wherever he goes, O'Leary follows. He wants Paul to be like him. Paul's like the son he never had.' She gave my arm a shake. 'He'll never let him go. Come down to the shelter with me and stay down there for the rest of the night. By morning it will be over, one way or another.'

'For Paul, too?'

Some expression I couldn't read rippled across her features. 'Perhaps.'

'Don't you care?'

Again that unreadable emotion passed over her face.

'Stay away from both of them.' She released my arm. 'Let's go down there.' She nodded towards a sign with an arrow pointing the way to a shelter.

I took advantage of her letting go of me to run from her, her cries for me to come back fading rapidly as I caught up with the guns and planes again.

Warmth from the flames on the buildings along Wardour Street stroked my cheeks like a taunting beast. A whistle alerted me to a prowling warden and I jumped into an alley to hide from him. When he'd passed I stepped back out into the street, not knowing where to go, where to find Paul Gabriel.

Something rustled behind me, audible even above the guns. When I turned I saw nothing. Probably just incendiaries again. I squinted at the shadows and recognised a C-shaped tail.

'Go away!' I told the dog. 'I haven't anything for you.'

He barked once and retreated into the gloom.

27

Searchlights picked out swarms of bombers to the south and gave me enough brightness to see where I was. Somehow I'd found my way on to Charing Cross Road. I walked north. At the junction with Tottenham Court Road and New Oxford Street I stopped, shivering in the chill but not registering that I was cold and couldn't feel my hands and feet.

A parachute flare glided down over Charing Cross Road, hovering over the second-hand bookshops. I still wasn't sure where to go but found myself crossing into Oxford Street and from there into Rathbone Place, following the latter till it curved into Charlotte Street. I knew these roads because they were so close to home and I'd played games as I cycled down them, counting the number of lampposts or trees or pillar boxes.

I stopped at the junction with Goodge Street, hearing something unexpected. Music. I turned in the direction of the notes. A violin played scales and arpeggios, the sound sometimes buried in the crashes of explosions and the pinging of shrapnel on to slate roofs. For a few minutes I lost the violin completely and stood still, turning my head from side to side like a wireless struggling to find a wavelength.

I caught the notes again and walked on towards their source.

An explosion in a nearby street splintered the notes and for a few seconds I thought the music had stopped. But when my ears stopped ringing I picked it out again.

I'd stopped counting lampposts and pillar boxes and making sure I knew which street I was on. The notes had seduced me away from my numbers. They'd also led me to the doorway of a shop. 'ISAAK CYRUS ANTIQUITIES'.

The door opened as I pushed it, no need to knock. I knew where I was now. Exactly where I needed to be if I wanted to find Paul Gabriel. I was standing in . . . what? A warehouse? Display room? Shop? The lights were off, except for the gentle hissing glow of an amber gas lamp, revealing a bookcase crammed with leather-bound books. An expensive-looking porcelain dinner service was piled up from the floor almost to the ceiling, cups and coffee pots and soup tureens sprawled over the rugged floor. I saw a chess set, snuff boxes, a doll's house. At any other time I'd have lingered by the books but the music drew me to the back room, more brightly lit than this foyer.

I walked towards the music. Standing in the middle of the office a violinist played, eyes closed, lips half open in concentration or enjoyment, I couldn't tell which. I recognised the elderly man who'd come into the Blue Lion with Inspector Blake. The inspector himself sat opposite, singing in a husky yet soft voice. Neither man noticed me come in.

The violinist played the last few bars, laid down the bow and smiled.

'I'm out of practice.'

'You play very well, Mr Cyrus.' With my newly sharpened eye I noticed how the relaxed air the inspector had displayed while he sang began to disappear. Had he sung to calm himself? Could someone as seemingly in control as Inspector Blake really need soothing? Perhaps I wasn't alone in needing distractions in times of strain. I gave my neck a scratch, out of habit, not because it needed it.

'The instrument is far too good for me.'

'Where did Gabriel steal it from?' I stiffened at the mention of Paul. They still hadn't seen me.

'From a solicitor's safe in Gray's Inn Road, where it was being stored for a promising young pupil at one of the London academies. I heard him play on this very instrument just a month before he was called up.' Mr Cyrus replaced the violin in the velvet-lined case. 'I didn't give Gabriel much for it, just five pounds.' Cyrus shook his head. 'So it won't be much loss to me when I return it to its owner.'

'You'll return it?'

'Do you think I'm completely lacking in morality, Inspector, just because I'm a pawnbroker?'

'You have to make a living. Five pounds is five pounds.' The inspector pulled out a wallet. 'I have some funds available.'

'No.' Cyrus shook his head. 'God knows, I haven't always been generous to customers in need.'

'You puzzle me, Mr Cyrus. I thought business was always business for people like . . .' He paused.

'Like me, you were going to say? Jewish people, is that what you meant? Or did you believe that money is the only important thing to people in my trade?'

The inspector flushed.

'In the latter case, you'd be right. That's how I used to be.' The shop rocked as an explosive landed nearby. 'How could I not, being what I am and coming from where I do? But people change,

Inspector.' His eyes took on a mischievous glint. 'And look, what a busy night I'm having. Now here is Miss Pearse come to join us.'

I stepped forward from the shadows, blushing.

'I felt a draught when you opened the door. I know your father. You have very similar –'

'Eyes,' I finished for him. 'Does everyone in London know my father? And what is it about my eyes, anyway?'

'They are an unusual shape.' Mr Cyrus waved me towards an antique mirror above the fireplace. 'Slightly slanted, feline, almost. Very attractive.'

I peered at my reflection and thought I saw what he meant. I liked the idea of myself as a cat, slinking through the streets with nine lives.

'Those of us in this carefully planned operation certainly *do* know your father, Rachel. And Mr Cyrus is no exception.' Inspector Blake shook his head. 'You were told to go down to the shelter. You've heard what it's like out there tonight.'

'I'm not alone in taking the risk.' I pulled myself away from the mirror and sat on a highly sprung sofa that threatened to buck me off. 'What's happening?'

I expected Inspector Blake not to tell me. 'We're waiting for Gabriel to arrive here with a valuable painting.' He looked directly at me.

ELIZA GRAHAM

'Because then we can arrest him. O'Leary will be along soon as well. We'll have both men and the stolen goods in one place.'

I started to protest. He lifted a hand to stop me.

'And if you do anything to try and prevent me, young lady, I will ring for a constable to come and take you to the cells. I don't often lock up fourteen-year-olds, but I will if you get in my way, Rachel.'

And this was the same man who'd been singing soppy songs just minutes earlier.

His expression softened just a touch.

'You'll remember me warning you on more than one occasion about that young man?' He pulled something out of his inner coat pocket. The ring. 'Did you read the inscription on this, Rachel, before you handed it in?'

I took it from him.

'*J. to E., 26.10.40*'. Just last weekend. The poor girl had only been engaged for a few days. My mouth filled with bile. I couldn't get around the fact that Paul had done something awful, something gruesome. The inspector wasn't telling me anything I didn't already know, but thinking about how he'd come by the ring made my stomach churn.

The inspector took it back from me. 'I know it was Gabriel who stole it because he was spotted at the nightclub when they were taking up the bodies.'

'But he gave it back!' I said. 'He handed it over to me to give in at the station. He knew it was wrong. He's sorry. Why won't you give him any credit for that?'

'Sometimes it's just too late for gestures.' Inspector Blake's tone was soft. 'It it weren't for the war perhaps we could take a chance on young Gabriel turning straight. But there's no time for that at the moment.'

'The country needs able-bodied young men. And he's strong and fit. He could join the army in a year or so.'

The raid must have quietened outside or else the bombers had moved away or something because a rap on the door made all three of us start.

'I'm coming, I'm coming,' Cyrus muttered. 'Must be Gabriel. Can't be that fool of a warden come to complain about my blackout, not a speck of light could get through my windows.'

Inspector Blake switched off the lights in the back room and pushed the door so that it was only open three or four inches.

'Not a word, Rachel,' he whispered. 'Don't attempt to warn him.' He sounded almost excited.

I sat back in my chair, arms crossed in disgust, racking my brain for ideas. There must be something I could do to alert Paul.

We heard claws scraping on the wooden showroom floor.

'Francis. You'll do yourself an injury running like that. You weren't built for speed.'

The dog was panting and so was the man.

'Not a moment to lose, Cyrus. Has Paulie brought you anything?'

'Nothing. Anything wrong, Francis?'

'I'm fine.'

I glanced at the inspector. Shouldn't he be marching into the showroom now to arrest O'Leary?

'Are you rushing off somewhere?'

'What's it to you?' The dog whined. 'If that young devil hasn't kept his word I'll take my leave. You can tell him from me he'll be sorry for playing games.' Again I looked at Inspector Blake. He stood motionless at the door.

The shop door squeaked again.

Cyrus came back in and switched on the lights.

'He's running scared.' The anti-aircraft started up again and he had to raise his voice. 'Are you going to follow him?'

'There are men out on the street, they'll keep an eye on him.'

'Why didn't you just arrest him now?' I demanded. 'You had the perfect opportunity.'

'We need him with the stolen goods or evidence that he benefited from the theft, like the money.' The inspector spoke patiently.

'But why? You've got enough evidence against him.'

'We haven't. We need to show he was the lynch pin of this particular racket.'

'What about all the spy stuff?'

The inspector shifted his weight from one foot to another.

'We can't prove anything against him on the security side, at the moment, but we can get him locked up for a long time if we can arrest him for major theft. Then he's likely to want to talk to help himself.'

'By major theft, you mean stealing that painting from Lord Street.'

He nodded.

'But you can only do that by making Paul bring it to him! That's so unfair. Paul didn't want to get involved with the painting. O'Leary black-mailed him.'

'Think about it, Rachel. What's the liberty of a young thief weighed against the morale of thousands of Londoners? Or the security of the country, if, as we suspect, O'Leary's been talking to the Germans? Can you really tell me that Paul Gabriel matters more than everyone else?'

'He does to me!'

'If you say so.' He sounded cold. 'I'm sure your parents would find that an interesting demonstration of loyalty. May I use your telephone, Mr Cyrus?'

'Please.' The older man pointed at the ivory receiver on the desk. He patted my shoulder. 'Please don't worry, Miss Pearse. I will talk to the inspector. He is softer than he appears.'

I tried hard to feel reassured.

The inspector had just reached the telephone when the lights went out.

'Must be a cable down,' said Mr Cyrus.

I took the opportunity to slip out into the showroom and through the shop door, the darkness enfolding me. I heard the inspector shout but I kept on running. I ran as fast as I could. I had to find Paul and tell him to dump the painting, to hide while he still could.

I came to a junction and halted.

28

Where exactly was I?

My haste to escape the inspector had driven me out here like a fox running from hounds, blind to everything else but the need to escape.

Something touched my shoulder.

'We're all going to die,' shouted a drunk over the scream of the bombers, breathing alcoholic fumes into my face. I pushed him off and ran into an alley, tripping on an uneven paving stone and throwing out an arm to catch my balance: saving myself just before I fell to the ground.

I came out the other end and found myself on a street I didn't recognise. I stopped to grab a breath. The drunk had unsettled me. How many lampposts had I passed? Postboxes? I hadn't been paying attention. I was lost. As the inspector had warned, dangerous gangs hung around here. If someone jumped you with a knife, the bombs and artillery would drown your screams. Nobody would come to your help. Until tonight I'd never taken any of these warnings seriously.

I'd somehow reached a wide road. Where now? Two fire engines shot past me. I was probably only about ten minutes from home. Perhaps I should aim for there, then I could find Lord Street. If Paul Gabriel was still there. If I wasn't too late.

I could see nothing to use as a landmark and turned left randomly. A shadowy figure moved out of a shop doorway.

'Got anything to spare, love?' He came towards me, hand held out. As he approached, surprise flickered over his coarse features. He hadn't been expecting someone my age. The cautious optimism in his eyes turned to calculating greed. He was at least a foot taller than I was. His eyes took on a sharp expression.

I jumped off the kerb to avoid him and crossed the wide road, turning into the first side street I came to. A searchlight briefly illuminated a curious mock-Tudor shed in the middle of a square and I knew I was in Soho, very close to Oxford Street. I worked my way to what I thought was the north of the square, using what remained of the fence round the little park to keep on course.

I reached a strip of emptiness and had to let go of the railings and launch myself into it, like a diver plunging into inky depths, my blackout torch providing only the faintest glow

A single car threw feeble lights along a dark strip. I turned off my torch in case it was the inspector again. I'd reached what I was sure was Oxford Street, but I couldn't work out how far north I was. Had I run two blocks south or twenty?

A searchlight sketched an arc across the inky sky and picked out the words 'Walton Old Queen's Head' on a wall high above me. I knew this building. It faced Oxford Street opposite Rathbone Place. Since I'd picked up the first notes from Mr Cyrus's violin I'd almost made a huge circle.

I crossed the wide road again, darkness enclosing me. I must be close to both Lord Street and our flat. Paul must be somewhere around here. If I could just intercept him.

My coat was warm but I shivered. I'd never felt like this about the night before. Bodies seemed to call out to me from the rubble. The rescue teams couldn't find everyone who'd died, could they? Were there still people alive under those scorched bricks? Or worse, did people lie in the ruins who'd been killed so suddenly that they didn't realise they were dead? I wished now I could forget a story Mrs H had told me about a photographer who'd claimed she'd seen white shapes in the photographs of vacant bombed buildings she'd developed, white shapes that hadn't been there when she'd taken the pictures. Ghosts.

I increased my pace, trying to outrun my fear before it could grip me round the throat and overwhelm me.

The planes were still coming in waves. Surely they'd run out of bombs soon, or were the Germans going to keep coming until they'd killed every living creature in London? Movement was the only way to keep panic at bay. All my brave words about finding the bombing exciting – they'd been lies.

I felt as though I was the only living creature on the ground.

I turned a corner and right in front of me there was a ghost on the first floor of a bombed-out house, beckoning me with its white flashing arms. I screamed but a plane whined low and the sound of my terror was lost.

But it wasn't really a ghost – just a tall mirror swinging in the vibrations of the guns and bombers, reflecting the glare from the search-lights and throwing it back on to the street. Only a mirror. I told my legs to stop running but they wouldn't listen. Where was I? I slowed and realised I was halfway down Outcast Street and needed to head north. I turned right, hoping I'd come out into Mortimer Street opposite the Middlesex Hospital.

A warden emerged from the gloom, starting at me as though I were a creature from another world. I jumped out of the way. A bomb whistling down pushed all the air away from us. A big bomb. Too close. I closed my eyes and waited for extinction. The ground shook. Glass crashed out of windows behind me. This must be death coming for me. When I looked again the warden and I were standing in the middle of a sea of glass and rubble. I put a hand to my hair to brush out the shards, then realised I'd lacerate my hands. So I closed my eyes and shook my head from side to side like a wet dog, little pieces of glass tinkling on to the pavement.

'What the hell are you doing out here?' The warden started dragging me towards a church. 'Get down into the crypt. If I find you up here again I'll have you charged, you silly bloody kid.'

'Rachel!' Paul Gabriel's voice. Using some superhuman strength I pulled myself away from the warden. Paul was coming towards me through the smoke, his eyes bright, something large and rectangular in his arms. The painting.

'In there now, before I call the police.' The warden's face was puce.

'Are you all right?' Paul was asking me. 'Where've you been?' A second explosion threw a wave of light over the street.

And I was asking him the same things and we couldn't hear one another because the warden was still yelling and the guns were still blazing. The warden shoved me down the steps towards the crypt but he couldn't get hold of Paul, who was backing away. Across the street the glass front of an office fell in and a flurry of papers swirled into the sky, flak illuminating them so they looked possessed by an invisible demon.

'Come on!' I tried to grab his hand. 'Let's get down here.'

'No.' He was shaking his head, looking over my shoulder at something I couldn't see, just as he had that very first time we'd met. 'I can't stay with you. I've got to sort this out.'

'Give me that.' I tugged the painting out of his hands. 'If you haven't got it on you they can't prove a thing, not even the ring.'

'They know it was me who took that ring?' He swallowed. 'I thought they'd work that one out.' He was walking away from me.

'Come back,' I screamed again as a flare lit the street, revealing the inspector's black car. By now the strength was leaving my body and the warden could grapple me down the steps.

'Stay down here,' he shouted. 'Or by God I'll make you sorry.'

He shoved me down on to a bench between two children. I forced myself to take deep breaths, to calm down. The canvas-wrapped painting dug into my knees. It was heavy but I didn't dare put it down. This Dutch girl with her smooth skin and lustrous hair had caused so much trouble for everyone. Just like me, in fact.

The warden moved along the shelter to reprimand an unruly party of card-players. If I made a dash for the stairs to the street he wouldn't be able to stop me. But a solider in uniform reached over the kid next to me and tapped me on the shoulder.

'You stay down here, love. It's hell up there tonight.' His eyes were friendly but held a threat in them. He wasn't going to let me past him to the stairs.

I shrank back on the bench. It could be hours until the all-clear sounded. A middle-aged woman opposite me nodded in approval.

'Back in September I could sit down here for hours and it was just a bit of a laugh. But now . . .' She shrugged.

'The novelty's gone,' another woman agreed. 'Don't know if I can be fagged to come down here again after tonight.' She clutched a stout black handbag to herself as though it were a baby.

'Think I'd rather take my chances in my own house.'

'At least you'd know some bloody looter isn't going through your smalls while you're stuck down here.'

They prattled on about people they knew who'd had terrible things happen to them in raids: children orphaned, women widowed, homes wrecked and plundered. I let their conversation wash over me, falling into a half-sleep, only distantly hearing the card-players calling out their bids, barely noticing the warden's torch running along the benches, the explosions above. I dreamed my father was pushing Paul Gabriel into a burning doorway as punishment for painting a portrait of me without any clothes on.

The vicar appeared and offered tea and toast. I shook my head and muttered a thanks. The warden sat down for his refreshment. I waited until he was occupied with putting sugar in his tea and then I rose. Nobody seemed to notice. The soldier who'd detained me before snored gently. Clutching the painting to myself I walked up to street level. I rubbed my sleeve so I could look at my watch. I'd been down there for just over forty minutes, not as long as I'd feared. Strange how you lost touch with time when you were in a shelter. Fires burned around me and the air was thick with soot.

A car braked beside me.

'Rachel!' My father – with Inspector Blake. 'Thank God you're safe.'

'Jump in,' said the inspector. 'At least we'll know where you are then, young lady.' The uniformed policeman in the back undid the door.

'Here.' I shoved the painting into the car. 'This is what you were looking for. As you can see, Paul Gabriel doesn't have it. Your scheming failed. I took the painting. Leave him alone.'

A shell burst above us, revealing an axe swinging to and fro on the first floor of a wrecked house opposite. They used to chop off heads in the Tower of London. Traitors still went to the Tower but they shot them now, or dropped them through a trapdoor with nooses round their necks. They hanged looters too these days. Paul Gabriel was still in danger.

'Come on, Rachel!' Dad called.

I slipped back into the smoke, hearing their shouts but quickly becoming invisible.

29

Now I was closer I could see it wasn't an axe in the ruined house. It was a mirror in what had once been the bedroom and it was slicing the air as vibrations hit it.

'Rachel?' someone whispered from a doorway.

Paul.

'How long have you been here?' I was in his arms, his warm breath was blowing against my cheek.

'All the time you were in the shelter.'

'Why?' Had he gone mad? He could have been far away by now. I looked at his face and saw why he'd waited. Because of me. Because he was scared for me.

'It's been a heavy night,' was all he said. 'Even shelters aren't safe if there's a direct hit.' He released me. 'You should go back down there. Or home. Or even to the basement in Lord Street. That place is safe enough now the painting's gone.'

'I gave the painting to Inspector Blake. He's got nothing on you now, nothing. Run for it while you can! Let them forget all about you.'

'If the police catch O'Leary he'll sing and I'm done for. He's got stuff on me going back years.' Paul didn't even sound angry any more, just resigned.

'So get away now while you can. Run!'

He put a finger to his lips. Someone was coming. I strained my eyes to see through the haze and made out the figure in the green tweed with the white dog behind him, running like a wizard and his familiar. Then I heard something else: the purr of an engine.

'Run!' I hissed again.

Instead he pulled me back into the shop entrance. 'Let's see if they get him.'

The car came to a halt and the inspector and sergeant got out. The latter blew a whistle, presumably to attract other policemen working the streets. In a moment they'd find us and drag us off to the cells. But Paul could still get away, he knew passageways and alleys they didn't know. He could outrun them in the dark and make for that huge shelter in Tilbury where a man could hide out for weeks. Paul could still do it if he left *now*. I'd distract the police while he ran.

'I know where O'Leary's going,' he whispered to me. 'I know the route he'll go, too.'

'Don't waste time! Go!' I pushed him but he grabbed my hands.

'Listen, Rachel. If I lead the coppers to him perhaps they'll take it into account?'

'Are you mad? If you hand yourself over they're going to charge you with stealing a valuable ring, a violin and God knows what else. Aiding and abetting a traitor, probably.'

'I'm sick of running. I've been running for years, since Gran died.'

I clutched his sleeve as he moved out of the doorway, but he unlaced my fingers gently and walked away. The sergeant turned at the sound of his footsteps. Paul kept walking. Inspector Blake turned as well and in the gloom I saw the figures of three other policemen. Thirty yards. Twenty. Ten. They had him surrounded now. He couldn't escape.

'That way.' He pointed down the street. 'O'Leary's making for Euston Station. Probably wants to make his way back over the Irish Channel.' The policemen's hands went to their belts. I still found it strange that police carried guns these days. Now I found it positively terrifying.

Paul glanced back at me. 'Don't worry, Rachel.'

'Follow me,' he told the policemen as they came nearer. 'I'll lead you to him.' The droning planes had moved south now and the guns had stopped firing. I could hear every word he said.

'As if we'd trust scum like you,' sneered the sergeant. 'Cuff him.' Two constables moved towards Paul.

Inspector Blake stepped forward as they grabbed him.

'Paul Gabriel,' he mocked. 'Well, well. What's this all about, this sudden desire to help us? Sudden pricking of your conscience?'

'Why not? I gave you back the ring, didn't I? You have the painting too. We're wasting time, Inspector. O'Leary'll get away on the train. He's got false passports and ID. He'll hide out in some big northern city until you stop watching the ports and then you'll lose him to Dublin.'

'We're rather keen to talk to you as well, Mr Gabriel.'

'I'm the monkey, he's the organ-grinder. I promise I'll find him for you. And no trouble. I give you my word.'

'Your word. Who do you think you are?' muttered the sergeant. 'Let's get him into the car.'

'Sanders & Co. in Balham High Road. F. Hinds in Denmark Hill. J. H. Shakespeare in Leytonstone Road,' Paul said quickly.

Silence. The inspector moved closer. 'You know something about those robberies?'

'No. But O'Leary does.'

'He wasn't on the mainland then. The detectives handling those crimes made inquiries.'

'You never looked closely enough. He was here all right.' The inspector shook his head and then nodded at the policeman with the cuffs.

'That stabbing up at White City stadium? Remember that?'

'One of the gangs, probably the Hills.' But the inspector sounded less certain now.

'No, O'Leary. Billy Hill was visiting his auntie in Poplar that night.' I could almost hear the cogs in the inspector's mind whirring as he considered what Paul was saying.

'You're sure?'

'Yes. Easy enough for you to check, isn't it?'

A long pause fell. The bombers had moved so far away I could hear my own breathing now.

'All right.' He nodded to his companions. 'You find us O'Leary and we'll talk. No tricks. We're right behind you and we're armed.'

They moved off. I waited for them to get a few yards ahead before following the group.

As Paul crossed Charlotte Street the inspector's men were just a few yards behind him. O'Leary had a good start – precious minutes had passed since we'd first spotted him. But he was a stout man, not used to running; other people did his strenuous work for him. Gabriel broke into a sprint and the police followed. I kept as close as I dared. I thought I caught a glimpse of a white fleck. The dog's tail? A solitary Dornier buzzed overhead and covered the sound of my heels on the pavement. Surely Paul would be gaining on the Irishman?

I caught a glimpse of a sign. Rathbone Place again. O'Leary would hear them behind him, especially now the anti-aircraft guns had died down. He'd quicken his pace, duck into one of the alleyways, letting his followers overshoot him, while he cut into Tottenham Court Road. Would the inspector have sent men on ahead to Euston? Surely O'Leary wouldn't go there if he suspected he was being followed? He'd make for King's Cross or even Liverpool Street, over to the east, instead. Or hide away in some shabby boarding house for a few nights.

Ahead of me the group of policemen squeezed up against a shop window to allow a fire engine to mount the pavement, bells clanging. I jumped behind a pillar box in case they spotted me behind them.

In my mind's eye I scanned a map of Bloomsbury with all its shaded squares. O'Leary could be anywhere by now. Perhaps he'd doubled back and was sitting in some Soho pub or nightclub, laughing at the police.

Someone shouted ahead. Paul was running back towards me. I crouched as low as I could in my hiding place. Then, only yards away from me, he halted and seemed to vanish between two buildings. A passageway – so narrow you could pass it without knowing it was there. The police group followed, the sergeant warning them of danger.

Silence for whole seconds, minutes. Even the Germans seemed to be waiting to see what would happen because the whir of planes seemed to cease. Then a dog barking in fury, the crack of a gun and a muffled thump as something slumped to the ground. It was then I screamed, a scream which seemed to rip through the night, cutting through the whole world. O'Leary was emerging from the passageway with his gun held out and the dog straining at its lead.

'Drop the gun or we'll fire,' the inspector shouted. But he was still coming towards them, towards me. He'd spotted me. A faint smile creased his face. The gun tilted towards me.

'Come any closer and I'll shoot the girl.' He gestured with his gun for me to come out of my hiding place. I stood, legs shaking. The dog had seen me now and a low growl rumbled from its jowls as it remembered me.

Suddenly a small shadow detached itself from the gloom and launched itself at the dog. My stray, snarling and growling like a Fury. In the confusion O'Leary must have dropped both lead and gun because the two dogs rolled out into the gutter to continue the fight and O'Leary was scrabbling on the pavement for his weapon. His hand had reached it, but Inspector Blake was upon him, kicking it out of his reach.

And I was flying through the group of policemen who'd run to catch O'Leary and lock cuffs round him, dodging their outstretched arms, into the passageway, coming to a dead end at the back of some warehouses. Where Paul had cornered O'Leary for the inspector.

He lay on the cobbles like a crumpled grey blanket, looking smaller than he had done just minutes ago, like a young boy, which, I suppose, was all he was really. I fell to my knees beside him.

'Paul! Can you hear me?' I touched his cheek, still warm. Could I detect a flicker of life in his wide-open eyes?

I felt a tug on my sleeve and heard someone mutter in Yiddish. Mr Cyrus.

'I followed the inspector, too, Rachel.' He shook his head. 'Paul Gabriel never deserved this.'

'Stand back, Rachel.' Inspector Blake was here, too. He pulled me to my feet. 'Call for an ambulance,' he told one of the uniformed constables.

'Some hope on a night like this.' The constable waved a hand at the searchlights still arcing over the sky and ran off. Inspector Blake took off his overcoat and wrapped it over Paul.

'Young idiot. He should have waited until we'd caught up with him, not tackled O'Leary on his own.'

'He wanted to make sure you'd get him.' The tears were dropping on to my hands like drops from an icicle. 'He didn't want you to lose him.'

'Well, we haven't.'

'Is he . . . ?' The words caught in the back of my throat.

He stooped again and put a hand on Paul's neck. 'I'm not sure.'

An ambulance bell clanged in the street. It must have been already on the way to pick up a casualty. 'Wave them down,' Inspector Blake ordered, shouting for someone to bring torches.

Cyrus lit a match, knelt and examined Paul. 'His mouth moved, I thought.' He felt for a pulse in Paul's wrist. 'I think he's still alive. Can you see where he's bleeding from?'

'Out of the way.' A young woman in uniform was pushing the three of us aside and crouching beside the body. 'We've already got a casualty who needs to get to hospital immediately. Let me have a look.' She tilted back his mouth and put her ear to it and put a hand to the pulse on his wrist. 'He's definitely breathing but he's losing consciousness. Stretcher!' she shouted over her shoulder towards the ambulance. 'Quick as you can.'

'Shoo,' said Cyrus, waving his arms at something. 'Go away.' I turned and saw my stray watching us. He gave a single wave of his curved tail.

'Let him stay,' I said. 'He took out Flynn and held up O'Leary. He's on the same side as us.'

30

Two days later we had the funeral.

I think Dad thought it would take my mind off everything to arrange a little ceremony for Perseus, a bit like when I was a kid and he thought that a picnic in Richmond Park would make me forget yet another bad week at school.

He'd gone to some trouble with the burial arrangements, tying a purple ribbon around the shoebox that held the body of the departed, buying daisies from the market and digging a little hole in the dusty rectangle that was our communal back garden.

Mrs H looked remarkably perky. In fact, she seemed to think it was me who needed cheering up. I kept telling her I was fine. And I actually almost was. Paul was recovering in hospital – the inspector had telephoned to check on him this very morning. For one who'd been so determined to stick Paul into prison, Inspector Blake was being very thoughtful. He told me that the doctors had concluded that what had saved Paul from the bullet had been a tobacco tin filled with a substance they couldn't identify in the breast pocket of his overcoat.

Mum was still in hospital, but recovering more quickly now. At least I could visit her. Paul wasn't allowed visitors as he was technically under arrest, if you can be such a thing while you're in a hospital bed.

'You say a few words for Perseus, Rachel,' Mrs H said, as we stood round the tiny burial hole. 'You'd do it better than I.'

My lips opened to tell her that I couldn't, that I didn't feel up to it, but I found myself moving forward.

'Perseus, may you perch for eternity on a sunny branch with lots of people to sing and chatter to.' I bent down and threw a handful of dirt on to the shoebox. 'Ashes to ashes, dust to dust.'

Leander, as I'd christened the stray, lifted his head and howled like a wolf.

'Eva?' A long shadow fell over us.

Mrs H turned and let out a shriek and threw herself at the tall figure in a once-smart-but-now-shabby overcoat who was carrying a battered suitcase.

'Ernst!' Then they were rattling away in German and threatening to break one another's ribs in huge hugs. Dad and I exchanged glances and decided to leave them alone in the little back yard. The clouds moved away to allow a thin late-autumn sun to shine over the reunited couple.

'Was that Inspector Blake's doing?' I asked as we walked in through the back door, Leander bounding ahead. Dad grinned.

'I couldn't possibly say, but I think he had his doubts as to whether a Jewish gentleman with a bad chest in his late fifties constituted a security threat. Others may have shared the doubts.'

So I knew it had been the inspector.

'Young Gabriel's still on your mind, isn't he?' Dad squeezed my shoulder. 'I don't know how police and courts work, but it must count in his favour that he helped catch O'Leary.'

'Presumably that man's in prison now?'

Dad nodded. 'I heard they'd taken him to a country house in one of the suburbs, quite close to where we used to live, in fact, where they interrogate spies.'

I shivered.

'Not that O'Leary's exactly the international spymaster he fancies himself. I can't tell you much – I don't actually know much – but the inspector told me he's small fry, although he knows some interesting people. Putting characters like him away is always good for morale. And we need all the morale we can get at the moment.'

I longed to ask my father about himself, about his role in all this, whether the story about him joining the Blackshirts had all been complete fabrication. As though reading my mind he paused at the threshold of our flat.

'You've been very discreet about not asking me too many questions, Rachel. I'm impressed.' He unlocked the door. 'As I said before, there's a maturity to you these days. Clearly you were right not to accept that school we chose for you.'

My cheeks felt hot. He led the way into the living room. Leander followed us. He'd made himself very comfortable since we'd taken him in. Dad was going to take him to Berkshire when he left for his new job.

'I was so worried when the inspector told me you'd got involved with Gabriel. God knows, London is dangerous enough without looters for friends.' He held up a hand to silence my protests. 'And then there was the stunt you pulled on the street when O'Leary nearly shot you. And the inspector's had reports from two separate wardens, both livid, detailing the anti-social behaviour of a girl who wouldn't stay in the shelter during raids.'

'Oh.' I examined my shoes.

'But perhaps the least said the better.'

'Is that how you feel about your past, Dad, least said the better?' I hoped the pleading tone in my voice made it clear I didn't mean to be cheeky.

He pulled his pipe out of his pocket. 'Neither your mother nor I could tell you what I was up to while I was away. We'd both signed the Official Secrets Act. We hoped I'd be back much sooner than I was, long before you'd found out about the internment camp. The intelligence people promised it would only be for a couple of months.' His expression darkened. 'They also promised to arrange things so you could stay in Putney, too, but then Dunkirk fell and a German invasion was expected any day. Everything was chaotic.'

'What did you do in that camp?'

He took a lighter from his pocket and stared at it.

'Irena let slip a bit about it,' I prompted him.

'Did she now?'

I didn't want to get Irena into trouble, even though I still felt suspicious of her, with her smart, Continental manners and clothes and her misty connection with Paul Gabriel. She had saved my life.

'She didn't say much but I know you were fishing for information, trying to see if people in the internment camp were linked to traitors.'

He lit the pipe. 'I didn't find out very much, to be honest. I think rumours of a fifth column of traitors are highly exaggerated.'

'Did anyone mention O'Leary?'

He drew on the tobacco, eyes slightly narrowed.

'So they did talk about him. Well, I hope they shoot him. What about Irena?'

'Inspector Blake has employed her for about a year now. They planted her in those lodgings in Soho so she could get to know Gabriel and find out what O'Leary was up to.' He paused and continued in a very casual tone. 'I think she developed a sisterly concern for him.'

Nothing like the feelings Paul and I had had for one another. I hoped I wasn't blushing. I felt bad. I'd been mentally accusing Irena of having designs on Paul. Unlikely, really.

'Irena apparently has a young South African fiancé in the air force.' He gave me a sideways look as though seeing whether I'd look relieved. I almost certainly did.

'Did you often meet up with her?'

'Just once or twice, to look at some photographs. I can't tell you more.'

They'd probably been studying photos of O'Leary. O'Leary operating under different aliases.

'I still hate the way you dragged Paul into this.' The words came out in a fierce hiss.

'It's wartime, darling. Boys his age will find themselves wearing uniform within the year. It's a dangerous world for all young men now.' Dad sounded sad.

'That's different. Fighting in the army or the navy or the air force is risking your life for your country, for a good cause. It's not like risking your life in a police exercise.'

Dad took another draw on his pipe. 'Perhaps the two things aren't so very different. Think about it, Rachel.'

He sounded the way he probably did when he was talking to his students, keen for them to work through an issue for themselves. 'Draw your conclusions based on observation rather than preconception or emotion,' he'd always said in his dry, professor's way.

'Perhaps the inspector's work was important,' I conceded. 'But I don't know if I like big things always taking priority these days.'

'I'm not sure I like it, either,' said Dad. 'I see the need for sacrifices, but I wish they weren't necessary.'

I think we both felt a bit closer to one another then.

31

I visited Paul in Kent today. I left London still a schoolgirl and returned to Charing Cross Station feeling old, at least seventeen.

The journey down to the borstal, the prison-cross-school for people his age, took hours because the army needed the railway to move tanks and guns. We were shunted into sidings several times to allow endless wagons bearing iron machinery to trundle past. I shivered in the unheated carriage despite my warm coat and gloves and the fish paste sandwiches and thermos of tea Mrs H had made for me.

I couldn't find a taxi when the train finally drew into the station. There'd have been an hour's wait for a bus. So I walked the two miles out to the institution, lugging the parcel I'd brought with me.

The guard who unlocked the gate gave me a quizzical look. Perhaps girls didn't come out here to visit often. I seemed to walk through miles of cabbage-green corridors, oozing with damp. The place smelled of cabbage, too, cabbage that had been boiled for at least a week, mingled with the odour of damp woollens and old socks. At least there weren't as many iron bars as I'd imagined. Of course, it wasn't really a prison, more like a very strict school or army training camp.

Inspector Blake had told me Paul had been lucky. They'd arranged things so that he was sent to one of the more enlightened institutions for bright boys who are still redeemable, as they put it, rather than one of the dreadful places where they beat them and make them do endless drill and brutalise them.

Paul's actions on that terrible night three months ago had counted in his favour when he'd appeared in court. And as Dad said, nobody wanted to deprive a fit young man of a chance to fight Nazis in a year or so's time.

Inspector Blake must have pulled more strings, arranging this visit for me and telephoning the borstal to ask if we could have some time alone with minimal supervision: something they wouldn't normally allow an inmate with a non-family visitor.

'This won't be a regular occurrence, Rachel. Don't expect to go there again,' he'd said, handing me the pass. 'It's time for you to forget that young man and move on with your life.'

There always has to be a bit of a lecture with Inspector Blake. But I was grateful, all the same.

A warder ushered me into a waiting room and a minute later the door opened and there was Paul.

'Hello, Rachel.' He spoke quietly but his green eyes still sparkled with their old vitality. 'How are you?'

I muttered something about being fine, suddenly shy and awkward and longing to scratch my neck. I counted down from a hundred in seventeens, very quickly, to calm myself. The warder suggested that we might walk round the vegetable garden and took us out of a side door.

'Half an hour,' he said. 'Stay in full view of the house. I'm trusting you, miss.'

At first I felt almost shy with Paul and could only stare at him out of the corners of my eyes while he walked me round the frosted allotments. He'd filled out a bit. Obviously the rations were more food than he'd been used to in London. His arms and chest looked strong under his borstal-issue jumper. He said they did a lot of digging. You wouldn't have guessed he'd been shot – there was only the slightest stiffness when he walked. If he hadn't had that tobacco tin filled with Battenberg cake in his pocket it might have been different. Paul Gabriel could be the only person in the world who owed his life to a slice of cake.

'Do they give you time to study?' I asked. 'That's what they promised.' I sounded more like his aunt than his – what was I exactly?

'Three hours a day,' he said. 'And sometimes I can read on at night. The warder turns a blind eye to the light. You can learn a lot in a short time if you really want to.'

'I brought you some more books.' I handed him the brown paper package. 'Algebra, of course. A science textbook my dad says is excellent. A book about the Napoleonic wars. And an atlas.'

'Thanks.' His eyes gleamed as he took the parcel. I knew then that he'd be all right. Anyone who feels like that about books will pull themselves out of trouble. That's what Mrs H told me. She was working with refugee children from Holland and Belgium. They'd found it hard to learn in English at first but now they were doing well.

'Education is power,' Mrs H had said. 'That's why the Nazis had to burn all those books and take control of the schools.'

'I can do quadratic equations now,' Paul went on. 'It's not the kind of thing you boast about round here, mind. But I like the beauty of them. I like the way you can sort out everything and make sense of it all.'

'I love them too,' I said. 'Dad found me a temporary maths teacher. Until I start at a new school. He used to be a lecturer in a Polish university. So I'm hoping he'll teach me lots of new things.' I wouldn't have admitted this hope to anyone else on the planet. Showing such enthusiasm for a subject could get you into a lot of trouble with other people my age. Especially with girls, for some reason. I didn't know yet what they'd be like at my new school, whichever one it was, but I was praying there might be someone who'd like the look of me.

Looking at the rough young men working on the icy vegetable garden, pausing occasionally to throw sharp glances in our direction, I reminded myself that nothing I had to face could be worse than what Paul confronted here every day.

'When do you start the new school?' he asked.

'As soon as possible. My father's looking for one. But it's hard. Most of them have left the city.'

'So you'll be moving from London?'

'Mum's going to look for a house when she's fully recovered. I'll board until then.' I noted how I said when, not if, she recovered. It seemed fairly certain now, as certain as it could be, that Mum was going to be fine.

'So no more Heinkels and Dorniers for you?'

I wouldn't miss seeing their ominous black outlines, hearing the drone of their engines as they approached with their bombs, to kill and maim us. 'It's dying down now, anyway. Haven't seen the Luftwaffe for a whole week.'

'Do you miss those nights?'

I shook my head. 'It was fun, in a way, to start with.'

Then the fun had gone and it had felt murderous. I still shuddered when I thought of the tricks my mind had played on me in the dark, and of the drunk man reaching out at me. And of the ending, with O'Leary and his gun.

Something was obviously on Paul's mind. He kicked at a clod of earth. 'Did Inspector Blake manage to give that girl's ring back?'

I was pleased he felt worried about it because it showed how Paul had changed, how keen he was now to do the right thing. 'The inspector found the pilot she was engaged to. He wasn't badly hurt.' Paul still looked sombre. Probably thinking of the young man's face when he took back the ring he'd put on the girl's finger.

'And he gave me back the money we gave O'Leary as well,' I went on, keen to cheer him up. 'And Mrs H's teaspoons, which O'Leary took from her flat.'

Paul brightened. 'Perhaps you'll be able to buy something nice for yourself sometime.'

In fact the shops were almost bare now. Even at Christmas, there hadn't been much to buy. My money was back in my savings account.

'Will you write to me?' The change of subject was so sudden I blinked at the question. For the first time since I'd met him Paul sounded unsure of himself.

I hadn't known whether or not he'd want letters from me so I hadn't sent any. 'Of course.' My voice wobbled a bit. 'I'd love to write to you.'

I took my hands out of my pockets and he took them in his and I felt his fingers stroking my soft, clear skin.

And then we kissed, ducking down behind the compost heap so the warder wouldn't spot us. Some of the boys saw us, though, and wolf-whistled. The smell of rotting vegetables wafted over us. We didn't care.

The End

ABOUT THE AUTHOR

Eliza lives with her husband and children and Scottish terrier dog in a cottage in a very muddy part of Oxfordshire, which means that the house is never as neat as it should be, especially as she prefers reading and writing to vacuuming floors. When she was at school, Eliza used to read novels behind her text books because they were more interesting than lessons. *Blitz Kid* is her first book aimed at people of about 12-plus who enjoy a bit of history and adventure. Eliza grew up in London, at a time when there were still old air-raid shelters to play in as well as the odd bomb site, all of which made her very keen to learn more about the Blitz. Visit her website at www.elizagraham.co.uk.

Made in the USA
Lexington, KY
04 July 2019